Red Lipstick Kisses and Small Town Wishes

ALSO BY KATHRYN KALEIGH

Contemporary Romance
The Worthington Family

Red Lipstick Kisses and Small Town Wishes

THE DEVEREAUXS

BELIEVE IN FATE

KATHRYN KALEIGH

Chapter One

"I just need them to sell their property," I said.

My cat, Medley, twitched his ears and blinked at me.

"I know. You agree completely," I said, tapping my pen against my desk.

Swiveling around in my chair to watch the traffic below on the Interstate 610 Loop, I slipped my sneakers back on. Traffic was backed up, barely moving. The evening sunlight reflecting off the hundreds of windshields.

Moving my office to my twenty-sixth-floor condo had been one of the best decisions I had ever made. When I had leased it, I'd known the second bedroom would be useful one day. I just hadn't known for what at the time.

Sitting in traffic for hours a day was a huge waste of time that I didn't miss even a little.

Turning my phone over, I checked the time.

Four thirty. That explained the traffic. Lost in my work, I hadn't even realized the afternoon had passed. The last time I'd paid attention to the time had been at eight o'clock in the morning when I sat down at my desk to work.

I hadn't been working here in my home office long. Two weeks since I'd left the safety of the corporate office to stay home and work. I still had to go in to the office once a week, but that was so much better. So many fewer hours commuting.

I still had boxes of books and papers I'd brought with me stacked along the walls.

My home office had floor to ceiling windows with motorized blinds that I never lowered. I watched the sunrise while I had my first cup of coffee and then at night, I looked out over the city of Houston with the skyline miles away, but still distinctive.

I especially liked the view from my bedroom where I fell asleep watching cars' headlights flowing steadily. Since I was a little myopic, the lights glowed softly and sometimes I imagined the cars—actually on overpasses—traveling up and down mountainsides in and around Whiskey Springs where I had spent the summers of my youth.

At the sound of a message popping onto my computer screen, I swiveled back around and clicked ACCEPT.

My boss. Clara Miller was a boss that no one liked. Everyone at the office was certain that she had been a mean girl growing up. A mean girl who never grew out of her mean girl phase.

Another reason to be away from the office. Being away did not, however, keep her from pestering me. Anytime she took a whim to check in on me, she expected me to be sitting at my desk.

She had checked in several times a day when I first started working from home. Then, I guess she got bored with it since I was always at my desk where I was supposed to be and only checked once a day. This was the third time today.

My psychology professor would call it spontaneous recovery.

"Hi Ms. Miller," I said. She wanted us to call her Clara, but I insisted on calling her by her last name.

"Ava," she said without preamble. "Where are you on buying the Sterling building?"

Nowhere. "I'm working on it," I said.

"So no progress," Ms. Clara Miller said.

If she hadn't been looking right at me, I would have made a face. Instead, I smiled.

"Some progress," I said, holding up a legal notepad where I had scribbled copious notes. "Several dead ends, unfortunately."

"How hard can it be to find the owner of one house in Houston?"

Harder than you think. "It's hidden under a closely held corporation. I've gotten that far, but it's not easily accessible."

"I let you work from home because you're good at what you do." Ms. Miller glared at me through the computer.

How was I supposed to answer that?

"I'll figure it out," I said.

"If I recall, you told me the same thing this time yesterday."

She wasn't wrong. I had indeed told her the same thing yesterday.

So I didn't answer.

"I'll find out," Ms. Miller said. "And when I do, I want you to bring the sale home."

She logged off without so much as a see 'ya later.

The wicked witch of the west. That's what some of the other office workers called her. I tried to avoid name calling. I liked to hold myself to a higher standard.

It wasn't my fault the nickname came to mind at the moment.

A nickname like that had to be earned, after all.

I closed my computer and to go downstairs for a bottle of water. Medley jumped off his place behind my computer and followed me downstairs. Behind my computer was his favorite place to spend his days sleeping. It was almost like he was silently taunting Ms. Miller. She would never know he was there. It would be our little secret.

I'd been on this quest to find out the identity of the owner of the Sterling building for two days. Clara Miller wasn't going to just come back with it today.

She'd encounter all the same dead ends I had. And, having very few interruptions, I had the advantage, Ms. Miller notwithstanding. Ms. Miller, no doubt had lots of interruptions.

As I pulled a tumbler from the cabinet, Medley sat down and looked up at me.

"Low blood sugar?" I asked.

He meowed once.

As I pulled out a can of cat food and popped the lid, he purred and walked around me.

I set his plate of food down and filled my own tumbler with ice and water from the tap.

While I drank the cold water, Medley lapped up his gravy and salmon.

I glanced at my sports watch. I needed to get in some steps. But first maybe I'd order in.

The kitchen was a place for warming food and feeding Medley.

As far as actual cooking went, I figured that's what restaurants were for. Restaurants were the experts and they had the bandwidth for food prep. I did not.

First I would have to go to the market. Then I'd have to spend hours prepping. And cooking. Or baking. Or whatever the recipe required. Speaking of recipes, I'd have to find one of those first.

I liked the way my kitchen looked. Clean. Nothing on the cabinets other than a vase of fresh white daisies and one of those big jar candles with three wicks that I lit, usually at night.

I sat down at one of the bar stools and opened my phone to flip through my favorite delivery places trying to decide what to order for dinner.

A text message from Clara Miller came in interrupting my task.

She followed me everywhere.

> CLARA MILLER
> I found the owner.

> No way. How?

> CLARA MILLER
> I have my ways.

I didn't believe her. There were too many dead ends. No way she hadn't run up against them.

> Who?

When the answer came, I was glad I was sitting down.

CLARA MILLER

Rebecca Devereaux

I stared at the phone.

CLARA MILLER

Rebecca Devereaux of Maple Creek.
You probably know her.

Of course I knew Rebecca Devereaux of Maple Creek. The irony of all ironies. I had grown up in the small town of Maple Creek just north of Houston.

Maple Creek was a lot like a smaller—much smaller—small town version of The Woodlands in that it was well... wooded. It was different from The Woodlands though in that everyone knew everyone else.

My high school graduating class had consisted of eighty-six people. Eighty-six. I had been valedictorian. Other than being head of the journalism club, I hadn't taken part in any extracurricular activities. I had not been a cheerleader or in the band. Instead, I had taken college courses starting my junior year.

I had my MBA by the time I turned twenty-years-old.

They said I was precocious. I saw myself as being driven and goal-oriented.

I left Maple Creek, happy to see it in my rear-view mirror.

And I had not been back since the day I'd left for college.

I'd been raised by my aunt and uncle after my mother abandoned me as an infant.

My aunt made sure I was fed and clothed and taken care of, but she left no doubt in my mind that the only reason she allowed me to stay was because of my father.

My father's sister was my mother and my aunt, even though she never came right out and said it, didn't like the idea of another mouth to feed who wasn't her own flesh and blood.

She had three boys of her own and she doted on them. I was an inconvenience.

Somewhere along my teenage years, I'd made a vow to myself that I would never be someone else's burden.

But that wasn't the only significant thing about going back to Maple Creek after all these years.

There was most definitely more.

Chapter Two

AUSTIN DEVEREAUX

I turned off the autopilot and prepared to land the sleek Phenom airplane.

My copilot, a Labrador retriever with a sleek black coat, was on alert, watching out the front of the airplane.

He was a good copilot. Didn't require me to make small talk and didn't complain.

It was going to be a visual landing with no control tower to direct me in and no staff on the ground.

A perfect day for a flight. Cumulous clouds here and there dotting an otherwise clear blue sky.

I saw the postage stamp of a runway and steeled myself.

It wasn't the small deserted runway that bothered me.

I'd landed on smaller runways many times over.

As a pilot for Skye Travels, I went wherever I was needed and today I was needed to deliver a guide dog.

Although I was a pilot for Skye Travels, I worked specifically for Ainsley Worthington. Daughter of the founder of Skye Travels, she had started her own company beneath the umbrella of Skye Travels.

She delivered animals, mostly guide dogs to people who needed them.

I found it to be a rewarding job in and of itself on top of the already rewarding job of just getting to be a pilot.

I'd known I wanted to be a pilot since I was five-years-old when my grandfather had taken me to the Houston airport and we'd spent the better part of a day just watching airplanes take off and land. It had probably only been a couple of hours, but to me as a five-year-old, it had seemed like forever.

I may have only been five, but I still remembered what he had told me.

"Learn to fly airplanes, Grandson, and the world will open up to you in every way. You'll always be able to get work and you can go anywhere you want to go."

Grandpa, although he had always wanted to fly airplanes, had never done it. He'd stayed far too busy building and running his real estate company. He'd been a passenger on his share of airplanes though. Commercial planes. Private planes.

He was one of the most successful men I'd ever known. Much like Noah Worthington, the founder and owner of Skye Travels, the company I worked for.

They didn't make men like them anymore. The Greatest Generation. They were loyal to their country and they did what they needed to do to be successful.

Somehow they seemed to have more hours in their days than ordinary people. Or maybe they were just better at delegating. Grandpa always had time for me. That was something I cherished more than anything from my childhood.

I'd never gotten to ask my grandfather his secret for success. Something I regretted to this day.

But Maple Creek had been home. My mother, Grandpa's daughter, had married a small-town man and never looked back. They had raised me and my four siblings right here in Maple Creek and no one had known just how successful my Grandpa had been.

Hell, I hadn't known it until I was in college after Grandpa had passed.

I'd been just an ordinary boy growing up in a small-town.

Ordinary until that day in seventh grade when I had fallen head over heels in love with Ava Whitmore.

I remembered the day like it was yesterday. She'd kissed me.

It had been what my teachers called "Retro Day." I vaguely remembered her wearing rolled up blue jeans and an oversized sweatshirt. But the image burned into my brain was of her wearing deep red lipstick, the kind that had that distinctive scent found only in the reddest lipstick. It was one of those scents I would never stop associating with her. She'd kissed me on the cheek, leaving behind a lip imprint that I hadn't washed off until the next morning. And then only because it was smeared and I had to go to school.

For a thirteen-year-old boy being kissed by the hottest thirteen-year-old girl in the school changed my life forever.

She had, metaphorically of course, taken me by the shoulders and pointed me in what I now knew was the right direction.

I'd followed her to college, but she'd been so far ahead of me, I had been left in her dust.

She was taking college classes junior year so by the time we started college, she was a junior and I was still a freshman.

By then it didn't matter though.

By then we—meaning she—had already deemed it impossible for us to have a real relationship.

I had no reason to be nervous coming back to Maple Creek. There was one thing for certain. Ava Whitmore would not be here. She had left Maple Creek and had never looked back.

But anytime I came back to visit, which was rare, I felt enveloped in memories of Ava. Every step I took in the little town came with a memory of Ava.

I might have left Maple Creek behind, but I had never stopped being in love with Ava Whitmore.

There were two constants in my life. One was flying. And second was that Ava Whitmore would always be the love of my life.

It didn't even matter that I hadn't seen her in just over five years.

Chapter Three

AVA

The next morning I sat in Ms. Miller's office. It wasn't my day to go in to the office, but the situation warranted it.

Ms. Miller had been surprised to see me. Going in to the office on unscheduled days wasn't something I had done since I had started working from home.

I sat down in one of the soft leather chairs in front of her immaculately uncluttered desk with a glass top and spoke without preamble.

"I can't go to Maple Creek," I said. "You'll have to send someone else."

Ms. Miller narrowed her eyes at me. I didn't care if she saw this as a weakness. Anytime Ms. Miller caught any hint of anything she might see as a weakness, she would find a way to use it as a weapon.

Didn't matter. Going back to Maple Creek was not for me.

"I thought you would jump at the opportunity to go back to your hometown. Everyone wants to go back to their hometown. And getting to go for work is just a bonus." She smiled at me. "Right?"

"Trying to get Rebecca Devereaux to sell her property puts me in a double bind."

"Well," Ms. Miller said. "We all have our problems."

"I thought you wanted her to sell us this property."

"You know I do."

"I'm not the one to do it. She knows me."

"And she trusts you."

And therein was the heart of the problem.

I loved my job. I really did. But sometimes I didn't like convincing people to sell their property so that my company could turn around and sell it for investment property. Someone's prized property would be sold for a parking garage or a shopping mall.

Often times they were happy and willing to sell. Grateful to get a windfall on land they weren't using.

I was okay with those situations.

In this one, however, I already knew going in that Rebecca would not want to sell. And me going there to try to convince her otherwise was not only a waste of time and energy, but I was pretty sure she wouldn't be happy to see me to begin and end it all.

"If you like working from home, you'll close this deal."

"What does my working from home have to do with it?"

"You know I was against it to begin with. I like everyone where I can see them."

She wasn't lying about that. It was why she liked to "pop in" on my computer screen several times a day.

"I do my work," I said.

"I don't doubt it," Ms. Miller said, leaning back in her oversized office chair. She didn't weigh over a hundred pounds, but the chair was suitable for a two-hundred-pound man "But. If you can't land this deal, then you aren't ready for the autonomy required to work unsupervised."

"I'm not exactly unsupervised," I said under my breath, then added louder. "You know I do my job."

She shrugged. "Suit yourself."

I could tell by her tone that she had made up her mind. She was sending me to Maple Creek whether I wanted to go or not.

"If I have to send someone else, then you'll be working out of a cubicle."

"You can't put me back in a cubicle," I said. I hadn't worked in a cubicle in years. I'd left my own office, with a window, to go to work from home.

"Don't say I didn't warn you," she said.

As thus I was duly warned.

After going straight home to pack, I was on the road to Maple Creek by one o'clock.

Chapter Four

AUSTIN

After I finished up my post flight checklist and got my copilot, aka guide dog, aka Scottie, out of the plane, I still didn't have a ride from the airport.

So I called my best friend from high school to come and pick me up.

Reggie had always been content to live in Maple Creek. I had, in fact, never known him to have any aspirations to leave. It actually seemed like he never even considered leaving as an option.

There were a lot of people like that. A lot of people were born and raised in Maple Creek and were content to live out their lives here.

I could not fathom the thought.

Scottie went on alert when Reggie turned into the little airport, rumbling along in his old blue pickup truck.

As the truck neared, Scottie let out a low growl.

"I know," I said, putting a hand on his head. "You've never seen anything like this old truck, but I promise you it's safe. Or at least as safe as it can be. You don't even have to ride in the bed."

Reggie parked next to my airplane, reached across the cab, and opened the door.

"Dog rides in the bed," he said.

"And I know you know better," I said as I held the door for Scottie. "This dog has more education than you."

"Figured," Reggie said with a shrug.

I tossed my luggage in the back, then climbed into the passenger side. The heavy door creaked as I closed it.

"Where are we dropping him?" Reggie asked.

"Good question." I unlocked my phone and checked my messages.

"Why do you even have a phone?" Reggie asked.

"I wouldn't," I said with all seriousness. "But I have to have it for work."

"I think you were switched at birth. Maybe with some kind of cave child."

"Jealous," I said.

"Of what?" Reggie asked, genuinely confused.

I just laughed. Reggie and I had always been tight, but it didn't mean we understood each other. In fact, I could say with certainty that we did not come close to understanding each other.

"This is Scottie," I said after reading my latest message from my client. "An acclaimed guide dog and apparently we are hosting him until his new owner gets back in town."

"Your mother will be so happy about that."

"She won't mind." I put a hand on Scottie's head. "Scottie is housebroken. Doesn't say much. And is overall good company."

"Don't doubt that either." Reggie pulled out of the parking lot onto the highway that led into Maple Creek.

"How long you staying?"

"I guess until I can deliver Scottie."

"Uh huh." Reggie shifted gears and pulled over on the shoulder to let a newer car pass.

"Ever think about getting a new truck?" I asked.

"Why would I do that?"

"Just a thought. Figured a truck from this century might help you get a date now and then."

"If you must know, girls like my truck. In fact, I had a date last week."

"You've got to be lying. I know that no self-respecting girl would go out with you in this truck."

"Who says I took the truck?" he asked. "Besides she runs just fine." He pulled back onto the road. "As long I give her the attention she requires."

"Sounds like you're dating your truck."

"Don't be obtuse."

I laughed again. In some ways it was good to be home. I missed my family and friends.

I liked coming home, but I was always ready to be on my way, back into the large, more exciting world.

Reggie turned off the highway and followed a blacktop road

about half a mile before turning into my family's circle drive. The blacktop road was lined with rows of maple trees that would explode into a magnificent burst of red during autumn.

I always felt a little tug of homesickness or maybe nostalgia when I got here. This had been home for the first eighteen years of my life. It would always be home in more ways than I could count.

"Need help?" Reggie asked before I opened the door.

"I've got it."

"Call me later," Reggie said. "We'll go sit on the water tower and have a beer."

"You make it hard to resist," I said, grabbing Scottie's leash and urging her out of the truck.

Reggie gave me a mock salute, waited for me to pull my luggage out of the back of the truck, then rumbled back down the driveway leaving me in a world of relative silence.

I stood a moment and looked at the house.

Someone had added a new coat of white paint to the outside walls and planted some petunias in the hanging pots on the front porch.

It looked good.

My mother and father still lived here with their three youngest. They were some of those people who would never leave Maple Creek.

"Come on Scottie," I said. "Let's go meet the family. Don't get too attached though. You won't be here long."

I don't think Scottie cared. He happily followed me up the sidewalk to the house.

The house had a wraparound porch, literally going all the way around the house. The upstairs had plenty of room, but no balconies.

When my parents had built the house, my mother was terrified that one of her children might go onto the balcony and jump/fall off. So no balconies.

So no balconies even though a veranda would have worked well with the style of the house.

I knocked on the door. I had a key, but it didn't seem right using it.

Didn't need it anyway.

My mother appeared at the door, grinned broadly, and pulled me into a bear hug.

"It's been too long," she said. "Let me look at you." Holding me at arm's length, she studied me.

"It hasn't been that long," I said. "I don't look any different."

"You need to eat more. You're too skinny."

"My pants still fit and my doctor says I'm good."

"Well, honey, your doctor is an idiot."

Yes. It was good to be home.

"Is this the one you told me about?" she asked. "Scottie."

Scottie barked once.

"He's a good dog."

"I'm sure he is," she said. "Your grandmother is here."

"What? You didn't tell me that Grandma was coming."

"And ruin the surprise. No way."

I went straight into the kitchen where I knew Grandma waited, Scottie at my heels.

Grandma's face lit up when she saw the dog. Since Grandpa's passing two years ago, it took a lot to get her to smile.

Scottie seemed to sense that and proceeded to lick Grandma's face, making her giggle like a schoolgirl.

"Can I keep her?" she asked.

"Unfortunately, she's already spoken for."

"A working dog, huh?"

"I'm afraid so."

"If you ever retire," Grandma told Scottie, holding his head and looking into his eyes. "You have a place to live with me. Don't you forget it."

Scottie backed twice.

If I had more time with him, I would figure out the dog's code and we could communicate.

In the meantime, I gave my grandmother a hug.

"I'm glad you're here," I said.

Grandma had a place near downtown Houston where she still lived. She claimed she never ran out of things to do and that's why she never left Houston. Not even after Grandpa passed away.

I was pretty sure she rarely got out anymore, but no one challenged her on that.

"Me too," she said, then leaned forward and whispered for my ears only. "I'm thinking about moving in. Here."

"You'd leave the city?"

She shrugged. "It's not the same anymore."

"I see."

"Your mother doesn't know it yet."

"I'm sure she'd be fine with it."

I actually had no idea what Mother would think, but it seemed like the thing to say.

"When?" I asked.

Grandma waved a hand. "I don't know. Haven't gotten that far yet."

"You'll figure it out."

Grandma smiled her small wistful smile. "I suppose I will."

I hated seeing her so heartbroken over my grandfather, but they had been a true couple. Meant for each other. If my grandma remarried, I would be shocked.

In fact, I would bet my career on her never getting married again.

"Did your mother tell you?" Grandma asked.

"Did Mother tell me what?"

"Ava Whitmore is in town."

Chapter Five

Ava

Ms. Miller's assistant booked me a room at the Maple Creek Inn.

I found that interesting that even though Ms. Miller knew that I was from Maple Creek, she didn't assume I would want to stay with family. That told me a lot. It told me that Ms. Miller had looked into my background. Either that or she had booked my room at the inn to be difficult. Or maybe her assistant simply didn't know I was from there and Ms. Miller hadn't bothered to tell her.

Whichever it was, it saved me the trouble of doing it myself.

I pulled up in front of the inn and parked. At first glance, nothing had changed.

The inn was just north of town at the edge of Main Street. Main Street still had about a million ivies in large wooden planters. The greenery spilled over the sides just as it had when I'd been here years ago. the plants might be a little longer, but they were just as green. I'd always thought of them as one of Maple Creek's downtown signatures.

Being here brought back a lot of memories.

Fourth of July parades with the fire engine as the main attraction. Watching my classmates marching in step, wearing their uniforms. Watching other classmates riding in their cars decorated with homemade flowers and posters. The homecoming court. The football team.

The journalism club never had a float, but I didn't mind. I watched from the sidelines and I was okay with that.

It was a nice break from studying without all the prep time that went into the decorating and such.

The inn was actually an old house. A two-story white house that had been here forever. It had actually been the Chamber of Commerce building a hundred years ago, but someone had bought it and converted it first into a house, then into hotel rooms. Most people didn't even know that. Only those of us who read everything.

I liked that they hadn't torn it down to build a hotel. That would have been the simplest thing to do. But instead they had preserved it and made it into something that a lot of people could enjoy.

My senior prom, in fact, had been held in the inn's ballroom.

Yes. Definitely a lot of memories.

Gathering my resolve to get this over with, I grabbed my purse and stepped out of the car into the September heat. Whoever said autumn was here just because it was September was not familiar with Texas.

Still. There was something in the air. A cool undercurrent in the breeze. It reminded me of how much I loved going back to school in the fall.

Fall meant new clothes. New notebooks. New classes.

Even now, when the end of August rolled into September, I walked wistfully past the school supply aisle at the stores, looking longingly at the rows of supplies and feeling like I was missing out on something.

Fall had always been a reset time for me. A fresh start.

Without that arbitrary delineation of time, the years just blurred one right into the other.

Maybe I should have been a college professor instead of an investment broker. Maybe I would think about that for later.

But I enjoyed what I did.

I went up the stairs and stepped into the welcoming cool air.

"Hello Ava," the man behind the counter said.

I stopped and looked at him. A heavyset man, he used his middle finger to push his glasses up on his nose. With that one small gesture, I immediately knew who he was.

"John Roberts," I said. "I didn't know you worked here."

"A man has to pay the bills," he said.

I nodded slowly, taking in the gray streaks in his hair and the wedding ring on his finger.

John and I had been in the same class. Nothing more than class-mates, but in a small town like Maple Creek, students got to know each other quite well. Sometimes too well.

"Did I hear correctly that you got married and had a baby?" I asked. I hadn't actually heard that, but I was good at reading people.

"Two babies." John beamed. "And one on the way."

"Wow. Congratulations John."

"Thanks," he said as he pushed his glasses up his nose again.

"What's it like? Being a father?"

"It's chaotic," he said.

"But worth it, right?"

"At least some of the time." But he turned a framed photograph around for me to see.

"You love it," I said. Over the years, I'd honed my observation skills. It was one of the many reasons I was good at what I did.

I also had what my psychology professor called grit. Once I decided to become a real estate investment broker, I learned everything I could about it—was still learning—and I kept going until I became successful. And I would keep going until I was my own boss.

That was one of the things I didn't like about working from the office. There was too much negativity. Too many people there just to draw a paycheck. I wanted more. I wanted to be successful at what I did. Not just to get by.

"Yeah," John said. "I do. How about you? Any kids?"

"Oh no," I said. "I'm not even dating anyone."

I was okay with my single life, but in that moment, I felt developmentally behind.

Should I be married with children by now?

I shook it off. I didn't live in Maple Creek and I didn't live their lifestyle. Get married. Have kids. Grow old.

I lived in the city of Houston. A place where being single at my age was more normal than having a family.

"Oh," John said. "Well. I got your room ready."

"Thank you, John."

As he tapped on the computer keyboard, checking me in, he looked at me over his glasses.

"Kind of surprised to see you here after everything that happened."

"What happened?" I asked.

"You know. With your aunt."

"What happened with my aunt?"

"You don't know?"

"I haven't kept up." I shrugged.

"She married that Boris fellow and they moved to Florida."

"Boris? Who's Boris?"

"You really haven't kept up, have you?" He printed a piece of paper and slid it over for me sign.

"No," I said, signing absently and sliding it back.

"Well." Warming up to the gossip, John leaned forward. "They'd been living together for two years. And." He held up a finger. "They sold the house."

"They sold the house?" I wondered if I should try to sound disappointed. Unfortunately, I wasn't able to pull that off. I really didn't care what my aunt did.

"Yep. Lock, stock, and barrel. I don't expect they'll be coming back anytime soon. If ever."

I wondered about my brothers, but, again, I didn't see the point in being nosy.

Now if I'd still had my journalism team from high school, I would have had a good reason to scoop out the truth.

Right now I just wanted to get into my room. Get set up and try to figure out what my next move was going to be with Rebecca Devereaux.

I had to do something. Claire hadn't given me a choice there.

The hard part was going to be figuring out just what to do.

I hadn't even known that Rebecca had moved to Maple Creek. As far as I knew, she had always lived in Houston. But again. Didn't keep up.

I got on the elevator with an old-fashioned porter I didn't recognize. He was younger than me by several years which was probably why I didn't recognize him.

"Floor three?" he asked.

"How do you know that?" I asked.

He held up a slip of paper and grinned sheepishly.

"I have a cheat sheet."

Of course he did. It was the way of the younger generation.

He took me right up to the third floor and the elevator doors opened.

"Oh," he said as I went to step off. "There was someone here looking for you."

"For me?" That was odd.

"Yes. I apologize for not getting his name, but he definitely knew you."

Everyone here knew me and apparently the rumor of my coming to town had gotten here before I did.

I was used to the anonymity of the city, but while I was here I would have to revert to my upbringing and recognize that everyone would know my business before I would. It was the way of Maple Creek.

As I stepped out of the elevator, I shrugged it off. I might know a lot of people who lived in Maple Creek, but I didn't know of anyone who might be looking for me.

It could be anyone.

As far as I knew, no one knew the real reason for my visit and I planned to keep it that way for as long as I could.

That would probably last all of about five minutes.

Chapter Six

AUSTIN

I walked along Main Street, Scottie running ahead, checking out every wooden box, sporting a fresh coat of white paint, of ivies. Somehow he knew he wasn't on duty.

Although I transported a lot of service dogs, I mostly just dropped them off to whoever was going to be their new owners. As a result, I wasn't all that versed in just how they worked.

There had to be some kind of signal that would tell them it was time to go to work.

I'd check it out on Google.

But right now, I was focused on keeping Scottie out of trouble.

Scottie was a highly trained and very valuable dog. From what I understood, it was hard for someone to get qualified for one and then it could take months for them to actually get their dogs and that was after both of them had spent a lot of time training together.

Being a pilot, though, I was used to being responsible so that part didn't bother me.

Besides keeping Scottie out of trouble, the other thing on my mind was what my grandmother had told me.

I still had a hard time believing it.

Ava Whitmire was in town.

I would not have guessed that in a million years. If I ever saw her again, and I'd always known I would someday, I didn't think it would be here in Maple Creek.

She lived in Houston now. I knew that much. And since I lived there, too, that was where I expected to run into her.

I even went so far as to go by the Maple Creek Inn to see if she was there.

Since John wasn't at the desk, I'd asked the porter. He, of course, being younger, didn't recognize Ava's name.

I took that to mean she hadn't checked in yet and might not even be here yet. Since I had flown in after picking the dog up in Birmingham, but Ava would have driven.

I was pretty sure my grandmother was going off information gleaned from Ava having a reservation at the inn. The reservation no doubt preceded her actual arrival.

Scottie was an attention grabber. If I'd been trying to find someone to go out with, Scottie would have worked quite well in assisting with that.

Danielle Barker stepped out of the General Store and nearly ran right into me.

"Hey Austin," she said with a huge grin. "I heard you were here."

"Word travels fast," I said. And her timing, coming out of the General Store just as I walked past was suspicious.

Scottie sat down next to my feet and watched Danielle warily. He didn't try to go up and lick her face like he did a of people.

I was learning that Scottie was a good judge of people.

Danielle, too, had been in our class. She'd been on the homecoming court. The first thing I noticed about Danielle was that she was bigger. Quite a big bigger. Seeing her anywhere other than Maple Creek, I didn't think I would have recognized her.

Instead of dwelling on Danielle though, my thoughts arrowed straight to Ava. I hadn't seen her in years. She stayed off social media or at least any social media I could find.

What if she had changed? What if she was no longer the beautiful girl I had fallen in love with in high school? Of course she would change. Everyone changed as the years passed.

It wouldn't matter.

I would see right past it.

Still. The thought caught me a little bit off-guard. Mostly because seeing Danielle brought the realization of how much time had passed front and center.

Was my life really all that much different than it had been nine years ago when I had moved away from here to go to college?

Sure I was a successful pilot working for the most prestigious private airline company in the country. Pilots, fresh out of college, lined up at Noah Worthington's door to apply to work for him. More so than even to commercial airlines. Skye Travels was that prestigious.

I had a condo in downtown Houston. All the trappings of success.

But.

At twenty-seven I was still single with no marriage prospects. Sure. By normal modern standards, I wasn't supposed to be married. But being here in Maple Creek, my brain automatically reverted to the values I'd grown up with.

Get a good job.

Check.

Buy a house.

Condos counted.

Get married.

Nope.

Children.

Not even.

And now Danielle Barker was standing in front of me, blocking my path. Right in the middle of my existential crisis.

"What's her name?" she asked, looking at Scottie.

"His name. Scottie."

"He's adorable. And he's devoted to you. I can tell."

"Yes. Well. We're just on our way home."

"I saw your mother the other day in the Piggly Wiggly. She told me you're still single."

Why was Danielle looking at me that way? It must be the uniform.

What was wrong with my mother?

"I'm single, too," Danielle said with a little laugh.

"You know," I said. "I don't tell my mother everything."

"Oh." Her face fell. "You have a girlfriend."

I looked over my shoulder, then lowered my voice.

"Engaged."

"Oh. She didn't tell me."

"We're going to surprise her. But I've said too much. I'm running late."

"Okay. Right." She stepped aside. "See you later."

Scottie and I hurried past the General Store. Leaving Danielle Barker standing there looking quite confused and not a little bit disappointed.

Chapter Seven

AVA

Even though I was back in my hometown, I didn't have time for nostalgia, even if I wanted it. Which I did not.

I was here to do a job which I also did not want.

Rebecca Devereaux.

Now that I had the information about who owned the Sterling Building, I knew what I had to do.

It didn't keep me from stalling a bit. I brushed my hair. Freshened my makeup.

I was about to go to the Devereaux house.

I had spent a lot of time there in high school. More time, really, than I had spent at my own home once Austin Devereaux and I started going together.

We'd broken up during our first year in college. Actually I had been the one doing the breaking up.

Since I didn't know what he'd told his family, I didn't know what I was walking into.

As I unpacked my suitcase, I searched my brain for other options. Other ways to approach the older Mrs. Devereaux.

I'd met her, of course. Had spent some time with her at family gatherings.

The older Mr. Devereaux, Austin's grandfather, had passed away. I'd only just learned that from the paperwork. I hadn't known it.

He'd been a very likeable man and it broke my heart to learn that he wasn't with us anymore.

I especially felt bad for Austin. The two of them had been close. Austin was close with both his grandparents.

Actually, his whole family was close.

His family was everything mine wasn't.

He had his parents, his grandparents, and four siblings.

One big happy family and they all loved each other.

It was no wonder I spent more time at Austin's house than I had at my own.

And now I was supposed to go there and buy the Sterling House from Austin's grandmother. For investment property. A downtown developer wanted to build something else there. Condos maybe. Shopping. Maybe even a medical clinic.

I'd never been to the Sterling House, but I'd seen photographs. It was a grand old house. Built in another time. Before Houston grew up around it.

I was actually surprised it had lasted this long. Didn't make me feel any better about being the one to take it down.

Now that I was away from the office, I could work at my own pace. Ms. Miller would be checking in soon enough. She'd want to know if I'd closed the deal already. She had very little patience. However, to her credit, I had seen her take her time when necessary.

I could stall.

And that, I decided as I tucked my suitcase next to the little closet, was what I was going to do.

I'd go visit the Devereaux's house tomorrow.

Nothing said I had to go tonight.

I opened up my computer and logged in to answer some emails.

As was typical, I soon found myself lost in my work.

It was six o'clock when I surfaced and realized I was hungry.

There used to be a pizza parlor a block or so from here. I headed out to see if it was still there.

It was still hot by all possible reference points, but it was a little cooler than it had been in the middle of the day.

Leaving the hotel, I went down the covered sidewalk lined with wooden planters of ivies. I wondered if they were the same plants that had been in the planters when I lived here or if they had been replaced. I didn't know enough about plants to know how that worked. What was the lifespan of an ivy anyway?

I heard music pumping from the pizza parlor before I reached the end of the block. If the people waiting outside to get in was any indication, it was still a popular place.

I gave the hostess, looking everything like a high school senior, my name and went back outside to wait. I found an empty bench next to one of the ivy planters and moved one of the ivy strands aside to sit down.

I thought about ordering a pizza to go, but since I wasn't working, I didn't feel like holing up in my hotel room.

I didn't see anyone I recognized. That was a little surprising. Somehow I thought I'd be returning to a time capsule where everything and everyone was just as I'd left them.

But even in a small-town people came and went. My own aunt had left town. I wouldn't have ever predicted that. I didn't think she would ever leave here. But she had moved on as had her sons.

I probably actually knew some of the other people here, but they would have gotten older and would probably look different. Same as me.

If anyone recognized me, they didn't let on. John, at the inn, had recognized me, but he'd had the advantage of seeing my name on the reservation.

I idly picked up the strand of deep green ivy and laid it across my lap. The leaves were big and the strands were long. I was going with them being the same plants.

With nothing else to do while I waited, I focused on figuring out how to approach Mrs. Devereaux. It was possible, likely even, that she wasn't even here. For some reason Ms. Miller seemed to think that she was living here with her son and daughter-in-law.

Ms. Miller was almost always right, but I rather hoped she wasn't. If she wasn't here, then I could drive back to Houston in the morning and we could continue our search.

I couldn't even deny that I wanted to avoid seeing Austin's family. I had nothing against them, but I was nervous that they might have something against me.

Even though we had only been in high school, everyone had assumed that Austin and I would get married.

I thought about that sometimes and I wondered if that was part of the reason why I had broken up with Austin.

I had loved Austin, but I had felt like my fate had been sealed. Like I didn't have a choice.

That had frightened me more than just about anything. It frightened me enough that I had broken up with the one man I ever really cared about.

Water under the bridge.

I had moved on and I was certain that he had as well.

Chapter Eight

AUSTIN

I quickly learned that just because I was home didn't mean that everyone stopped and changed their plans. My younger brother was a football player and tonight being a home game, the whole family loaded up in the SUV to go to the game.

After my encounter with Danielle, I didn't feel like going to the local high school football game. I didn't feel like making up more lies about my love life to avoid being set up with a local girl I had absolutely no interest in.

The only local girl who interested me had left Maple Creek the same time I had.

After about thirty minutes of rumbling around the big house, I was giving some serious thought to catching up with them when Scottie came up, sat at my feet, and barked once.

It took me a minute, but I realized he probably needed to go outside.

I hooked up his leash and we headed out for an evening walk.

The sun was setting, leaving behind far too much heat for my taste.

Since I lived downtown Houston, when I wasn't working, I just went to one of the local restaurants in the tunnels and avoided the heat altogether.

Becoming reacclimated to spending time out in the heat would take some time. I'd made the right choice, I decided, by not going to the football game.

By habit, I walked down Main Street, Scottie in the lead.

All the little shops had already closed up for the night, but the pizza parlor was still open. In fact, from the looks of things, everyone who wasn't at the football game was at the pizza parlor.

Maybe I could slip in, order a pizza, and take it back home. Surely there was something on Netflix to watch tonight.

It was funny, I didn't go out much at night, but I always knew that I could if I wanted to. There was always something to do in Houston. I agreed with my grandmother on that.

Being in Maple Creek put a spotlight on there literally not being anything to do. Unless one wanted to go to a high school football game.

Since there was a crowd at the pizza parlor, I almost changed my mind. Being the beautiful dog that she was, Scottie attracted attention. With her with me, there was no way I was going to be able to just slip in for a pizza and leave.

When Scottie stopped to sniff at one of the ivy planters, I stopped, too.

That's when I saw her.

Ava Whitmore sat there like a forest nymph, surrounded by green ivy strands. There was even one in her lap.

I blinked, thinking maybe I was hallucinating. Maybe I was imagining seeing Ava sitting in a greenery.

When she turned and her eyes locked onto mine, registering immediate recognition, I knew that I was not hallucinating.

She was really here. Enveloped by ivies for some reason. But she was here.

And she had not changed one bit. Any concerns I might have had in that area had been unfounded.

She was still the beautiful girl she had always been. Granted, she was a grown-up version of the seventh-grade girl who had kissed me on the cheek with red, red lips, but she simply looked like a refined version of the college freshman I had known. Her hair, instead of being pulled back in a ponytail, her hair was pulled back messily, in that stylish way girls did, with a clip.

I would have known her anywhere.

She was wearing a light green pencil skirt and a white top with strappy sandals.

Just as I had done when I had caught sight of her, she blinked and I saw doubt cross her deep green eyes. Eyes that were the same color as the ivies surrounding her.

The years vanished, folding back on themselves and I was a young boy again, basking in the attention of the hottest girl in school.

Scottie ran up to Ava and sat down in front of her.

Scottie seemed to have the same idea I did, but Scottie could get away it.

Still looking at me, Ava absently rubbed Scottie's ears. Lucky dog.

Chapter Nine

AVA

I wasn't sure which one caught my attention first. The man or the dog. Maybe it was the two of them together.

But when I realized that the man wasn't just any man, but Austin Devereaux, every cell in my body went on high alert.

The song coming from the pizza parlor speakers was an older song. One that Austin and I had slow danced to at our prom. What were the odds of that happening?

Austin wasn't supposed to be here.

About fifty thoughts ran through my brain at the same time.

Had he moved back here?

When had he gotten a dog? He had always wanted a dog and a cat. He wanted both and wasn't afraid to admit it.

Did he have a cat?

Why did I not like the idea of him having a dog or a cat?

For some reason, I'd always thought, unconsciously, that he would wait for me and we would get a dog and a cat together.

It was a crazy, irrational thought that I hadn't even realized was stuck there in my head.

But then his dog was sitting in front of me, requesting politely that I pet him. It didn't surprise me that Austin's dog was polite. Austin came from a polite, well-mannered family.

It made perfect sense that his dog would be well-mannered as well.

I scratched the dog behind the ears, but I found it physically impossible to look away from Austin.

I had imagined this moment—seeing him again—a hundred different times and a hundred different ways.

He looked away for a moment, frowned, then walked right up to me and sat down next to me.

"Hi," he said.

Then before I could respond, he did the unthinkable.

He kissed me.

I was stunned speechless.

I was even more astonished when he put an arm around me and pulled me close.

"The ivies suit you," he said, then leaned close and lowered his voice. "Will you do me a favor?" he asked.

"What?" It was the only word I could come up with in the moment.

"Just play along," he said under his breath.

"Okay." Truly. What else could I say?

When Danielle Barker stopped in front of us, I had an inkling of what he was about.

I don't think he ever knew it, but Danielle Barker had a huge crush on Austin in high school.

It was never anything I'd worried about. Austin had never given me any reason to doubt that I was the only girl he ever had any interest in.

Danielle put her hands on her hips.

"I knew it," she said. "It had to be you."

Since I was supposed to be playing along with whatever was going on, I waited for Austin to take the lead.

"Hi Danielle," he simply said, pulling me ever so closer against him.

"I knew it had to be Ava."

There was a slight bite in her tone, but then it was possible I imagined it.

If I hadn't gotten much better at reading people over the years, I would have gone with it being my imagination. As it was, though, I recognized a biting tone when I heard one.

"Of course it did," Austin said, kissing me on the cheek. "Always was. Always will be."

"Congratulations," Danielle said. "I'd stay and chat, but I have to run."

After Danielle walked away, I turned and looked into Austin's sparkling blue eyes.

"What was that about?" I asked.

"You just saved me."

"From Danielle? Seriously?"

"Yes. Seriously. She wanted us to go out."

"You and her?"

He nodded. "Weird, huh?"

"No. Not so weird."

Austin removed his arm from around me, leaving me feeling bereft.

How quickly my body had accepted him back. Just as though he and I had never been apart.

"What do you know that I don't?" he asked, lifting the ivy from my lap and draping it into the planter.

"She's had a crush on you since we were freshmen in high school. Maybe even before that."

Austin looked at me as though I had gone mad, then looked in the general direction Danielle had gone.

"Now you're just making things up."

"So what did you tell her? That we were still dating?"

"Something like that," he said, looking away.

"Something like that?" I repeated. "But not that."

"I didn't actually tell her. I rather let her make assumptions."

"What did you do?"

"She thinks we're engaged."

"Austin!"

"What? I didn't tell her it was you. She figured that out all on her own."

"You do realize how small Maple Creek is, right?"

"I told her no one knows. It'll be okay."

"It'll be okay until it's all over town. How will you explain it to your parents?"

"By the time my parents hear about it, we'll both be long gone from here."

"Well," I said primly straightening my skirts. "You're the one who has to deal with the fallout."

"It won't be anything to worry about," he said.

Men. Why were they so smart at some things and so dumb at others at the same time?

Chapter Ten

AUSTIN

"Are you by yourself?" I asked.

Scottie sat between Ava and me, looking like a sentinel, guarding us against anyone who might interrupt.

Ava narrowed her eyes at me.

"You're asking me that now?"

I grinned.

"Seems like as good a time as any."

"I think perhaps you're asking a little too late."

I couldn't tell if she was messing with me or if maybe she wasn't by herself.

"Do I need to fight for your honor?"

Ava looked blankly at me for a moment, then put a hand over her mouth and laughed.

"You do realize that you're the one who put my honor in jeopardy, right?"

"I don't know what you mean."

Ava shook her head. "Something is wrong with you."

"Yes," I said. "I've been told that before."

She turned away, but not before I saw the smile on her lips.

"So since you're obviously by yourself," I said, going out on a limb, not even caring if it broke. "Want to share a pizza with me?"

"Maybe," she said.

"Maybe. You really know how to boost a man's ego."

"There's something I have to tell you before I agree to share a pizza with you." She scratched Scottie's ears and Scottie lay his head in her lap.

"That sounds incredibly suspicious."

"It does, doesn't it?"

"I can't even begin to imagine what you might need to tell me that involves pizza."

"I'm a vegetarian now," she said. "I eat seafood, so I guess I'm technically a pescatarian."

"I see," I said, biting my lip to keep a straight face. "That is most definitely something I have to take into consideration."

She bumped her shoulder against me, the way she had done a hundred times, usually after I said something stupid or charming or stupidly charming.

"Well," she said. "You have to decide quickly because my table is ready."

"I can eat a vegetarian pizza," I said, standing up with her. Scottie got to his feet, too.

"There might be a problem though," she said, tilting her head toward Scottie, as though she might offend him.

"Scottie. No. Scottie's not a problem. He's got papers."

"What does that mean?" she asked on a bubble of laughter.

"He's registered."

When we got to the hostess stand, I opened up my phone and showed the girl Scottie's papers.

"No problem," the girl said. "Follow me."

We followed the girl to a booth in the back. She slid in on one side and after Scottie climbed into the booth, I slid in next to him.

I had to admit it was rather odd sitting at a booth with a dog.

"What kind of papers does Scottie have?"

"Scottie is a registered guide dog."

"But... Why do you need a guide dog?"

Before I could answer, the server stopped at our table to take order.

Chapter Eleven

AVA

Austin had always been a well-mannered gentleman, but it seemed he had developed a rakish side somewhere along the way.

It probably had something to do with being a pilot. Pilots had a bad reputation for a reason.

Even in his jeans and white button-down shirt, I could imagine that he would be handsome in his uniform.

He placed our order, then turned and smiled at me, showing just a hint of a dimple in his cheek.

My heart did a funny little flip.

Funny because I had moved on from Austin Devereaux.

I had, after all, been the one to break up with him.

Right now, though, I honestly couldn't remember why I had broken up with him.

Maybe there had been something wrong with me.

There had definitely been something wrong with me.

"Guide dog? You aren't blind." Was there something I didn't know? I searched his eyes, looking for answers to something I didn't understand.

"No. I'm not blind."

Relief flowed through me. For just a moment, I had been a bit worried that I had missed something.

"But at the moment, I am his steward."

"Wait. Scottie isn't your dog?"

"Nah."

I couldn't decide if I wanted to be happy or sad about this. I decided to go with sad, right now anyway. I could explore why I might be happy about it later.

"But I like him," I said.

"Everyone likes Scottie."

"Are you sure you can't keep him?"

"I'm pretty sure. Scottie is a working dog. And my grandmother has already claimed him after he retires."

"Your grandmother?"

I was suddenly jolted back to the reality of why I was here to begin with.

"Yeah, they fell instantly for each other." He looked at me sideways. "Are you okay?"

"I just." So Ms. Miller was right. Mrs. Devereaux was here. In Maple Creek. "I just haven't eaten all day."

"Why do you do that to yourself?" he asked.

"Do what?" I forced myself to try to keep myself focused on what Austin was saying.

"You've always had a tendency to not take good care of yourself."

"I think I do okay."

"Except for forgetting to eat.

"There is that," I admitted. And I found it rather endearing that he remembered my tendency to skip meals.

But that wasn't what had me disconcerted. What had me disconcerted was that I was sitting here with Austin, my ex-boyfriend and I was supposed to seek out his grandmother and convince her to sell her home to an investment company.

That was enough to tip a girl off-balance.

As if sitting here with Austin wasn't enough.

Chapter Twelve

AUSTIN

"So you never got a dog? Or a cat?" Ava asked.

She sat across the booth from me. Too far away if you asked me.

It was noisy in the pizza parlor. I didn't mind that. I actually kind of liked it. I liked the way the noise seemed to insulate us from people around us, cocooning us together.

But I wanted to be closer to her.

I'd had a very good reason for kissing her and it had worked. Kissing her had sent Danielle on her way, discouraging her from wanting to go out with me.

But kissing Ava had sort of backfired on me.

Now I wanted to kiss her again.

Kissing her again had been the most natural thing in the world and at the same time it was brand new.

Her plump red lids curving into a little smile as she looked at me had me nearly coming undone.

Since she had broken up with me, what was it, five years ago, I had been just riding along the surface. One kiss and she had pulled me right back under.

I was back down deeply besotted by her.

Maybe I'd never really hit the surface. Maybe I'd just though I hit the surface.

"No," I said. "I haven't been home enough to have a pet."

"That's good," she said. "So no girl waiting at home to take care of them while you're away?"

"No," I said. "No girl waiting at home."

She nodded slowly as though she was trying to figure something out.

"You always wanted a cat and a dog," she said finally.

"That's right. Why do you say it's good I haven't gotten a pet?"

She shrugged and changed the subject. "You like working for Skye Travels?"

"They're a good family to work for," I said. "I work for Ainsley in the Pet Travels Division."

"They have divisions?"

"They have one division. Ainsley started her own division delivering animals. Usually guide dogs."

"Is it common for you to be the steward?"

"Not at all. But I'm responsible for getting them to their owners. That's why I'm still here. Waiting for Scottie's person to get home so I can make the delivery."

"You like it."

"What's not to like? I get to fly animals around the country. Animals are pretty easy to keep happy."

"I can't see you having trouble keeping anyone happy."

"I guess I like my alone time." I smiled.

The server brought our pizza. It was served on a stand with a candle beneath it to keep it warm.

"This is different," I said, examining the stand. "Have you seen anything like this?"

"No," she said. "It's an ingenious idea."

Sharing a pizza with Ava was also an ingenious idea.

Now that I had found Ava again, I wasn't going to let her go so easily this time.

I just had to figure out how I was going to go about keeping her.

Chapter Thirteen

AVA

We lingered at the table long enough that Scottie jumped off the booth onto the floor beneath the booth and fell asleep.

I don't think he was supposed to be sitting on the bench anyway, but it didn't bother me. It was a whole lot cleaner than the floor.

"Where are you staying?" Austin asked.

"The Inn."

"Right. Your aunt moved away, right?"

"That's what they tell me."

Austin should remember that I didn't like living with my aunt when she did live here.

"It's for the best," he said. "So why are you here?"

And there was the million-dollar question. The one I didn't want to answer.

I wasn't about to tell him the truth. Not now. My business was with his grandmother.

I wasn't into high pressure sales techniques. I'd have a conversation with her. Find out how she felt about the house in Houston and go from there.

"Work," I said.

"It's what we do."

"Seems that way." I was relieved I didn't actually have to answer his question about why I was here.

"Can I walk you back to the inn?"

"It's not really on your way home," I said.

"Scottie likes to walk."

"Scottie does."

At his name, Scottie came out from beneath the table, looked at Austin and barked once.

"Is that his signal that he needs to go for a walk?"

"Seems to be. If I had more time with him, I'd figure out his codes."

We left the table, Scottie leading the way.

"You'll never be satisfied with an ordinary dog," I said.

"You're probably right. I like things that are extraordinary."

I looked at him sideways. "Like flying airplanes."

He smiled. "That's one thing."

He had most definitely become more rakish over the last few years. It was rather attractive in some ways. In other ways, it made me wonder what kind of lifestyle he'd lived after we broke up.

Maybe I didn't want to think about that too much.

It was startlingly quiet as we stepped outside, the music and conversation of the restaurant fading into the background.

We walked slowly along the sidewalk, Scottie sniffing at every wooden ivy box that we passed.

"Do you think these are the original ivies?" I asked.

"Ivies can live for at least a hundred years."

"Seriously? How do you know that?"

"I know a lot of trivial things that have no use in the real world."

"It might be trivial, but it's interesting."

The walk to the inn wasn't nearly long enough. We stopped just outside the front door.

"We're here," I said unnecessarily. He and I had been here before. The last time being our senior prom.

"Can I borrow your phone?" he asked.

"You don't have one?"

"Who doesn't?"

With a shrug, I pulled my phone out of my purse and handed it to him.

As he held it in front of my face to unlock it, I watched him with curiosity. I didn't know what he was doing, but I didn't have anything to hide. Not in my phone anyway.

Except maybe some messages from Ms. Miller.

"What are you doing?" Suddenly worried, I asked, stepping closer to see what he was doing.

As he handed my phone back, his chimed.

"Exchanging phone numbers," he said.

"Oh." I took my phone back with relief. "All you had to do was ask."

"Can I have your phone number?"

"I guess it's okay since we're engaged."

He laughed. Scottie barked twice.

I knelt down to rub Scottie's head.

"I have to go inside now," I said. "Be a good doggie."

Scottie barked three times and lifted a hand.

I put my hand in his.

"He does tricks," I said, amazed.

"You're right," Austin said. "Not an ordinary dog."

Chapter Fourteen

AUSTIN

My family had heard the gossip about me and Ava before I even got home.

My sister Anastasia Devereaux, Ana to most everyone but me, was waiting up when I came in the door.

"Hey," I said, dropping my keys on the little table in the foyer. "Shouldn't you be asleep by now?"

Ana, just one year younger than me, and I had always been closest. She and I had been partners in crime on more occasions than I could count.

Whereas I had moved away after high school, Ana stayed home, commuting and taking online classes. She was getting her masters now and she had never left home.

I didn't want to think that she would end up being one of those people who never left Maple Creek. She was just being smart by living at home while she went to college.

Setting her book aside, she patted the couch next to her. Scottie took that as an invitation and hopped up to sit next to my sister.

"I waited up so I could be the first to hear the scoop," she said after greeting the dog.

"What scoop?" I asked, sitting on the other end of the couch.

"Well. I heard that you're engaged to Ava Whitmore."

"How did you possibly hear something like that?"

"Melissa told me. Sarah told her who heard it from Mike who heard it from... someone."

"You are seriously scaring me right now. What you just said was frighteningly small town."

She smiled. "Well. Is it true?"

"No, it's not true."

Apparently I did not put enough conviction in my voice for her to completely believe me.

"But there's some truth to it? I know she's in town."

"How do you know these things? Never mind. I don't want to know."

"Grandma told me that part."

"Figures," I said, looking toward the grandfather clock as it began to chime the hour.

"You have to invite her for dinner tomorrow. Daddy's going to grill."

"Why?"

"Lawrence is coming home," she said. "You know how they make a big deal when Lawrence comes home."

She made a face that made me laugh. We all knew that Lawrence, being the oldest, was our parents' favorite child.

I could claim it was because he rarely came home, but then neither did I. So that wasn't it.

"Why would I invite Ava over?" I asked. "So you all can torture her?"

"You know we all liked Ava. You're the one who let her go."

"Wasn't my idea," I said.

"Still. You let her go." Anastasia punched my shoulder.

"Ouch." I winced. "Okay. You're right. I let her go."

"And you'll bring her over tomorrow."

"If she'll come."

"Give me your phone," she said, holding out her hand. "I'll text her."

"No," I said. "You can't do that."

Anastasia crossed her arms. "I know you won't do it."

"I'll bring her over."

"Good." Anastasia settled back, opening her book, obviously dismissing me.

"That's it? That's all you wanted?"

Anastasia looked up.

"You might want a heads up that Mama and Grandma are already planning your wedding."

"You could have gone all night and not told me that."

Anastasia just grinned. "I know."

As I headed upstairs, I mentally kicked myself. I should have known that Danielle had a big mouth.

"Don't say a word," I told Scottie. "And you're sleeping on the floor."

I put a blanket on the floor next to my bed. Scottie dutifully laid down on it.

Such a good dog.

But when I came out of the bathroom, Scottie was sound asleep stretched out on the foot of my bed.

Ah well. There was one thing I knew for certain. I was going to miss Scottie.

I usually remembered to plug my phone in at night. Since I wasn't one of those people who was attached to their phone, I worked to make it a concerted habit.

After searching my pockets, I realized I had left it downstairs.

Not a problem. It could wait until morning.

I was almost asleep when it occurred to me that I had left my phone downstairs with Anastasia.

If she found it, there was no telling what kind of havoc she might wreak, but it was too late to worry about it now.

Chapter Fifteen

Ava

Ms. Miller was leaving me alone. No texts. No messages. No calls. That in itself was strange.

The other strange thing was just how easy everything was falling into place as far as me meeting with Mrs. Devereaux.

I'd gotten a text from Austin at eight thirty last night inviting me to come to a cookout tomorrow with his family. It surprised me that he hadn't wasted any time.

This created a whole host of new problems.

I'd planned on just dropping by during the day when no one was home. Meeting with Mrs. Devereaux and getting it all over with.

But now the game had changed. Now I would be going over for a social visit.

This changed everything. I stood at my little closet and looked at the clothes I had brought with me to wear.

A quick glance at my watch told me that I had time to drive home, get a different outfit, and drive back. But that just wasn't logical.

First of all, I hated driving. The very reason I worked from home now and second, I wasn't sure I had anything I wanted to wear in my own closet.

I couldn't go over there to a cookout wearing a business suit. That would just be wrong.

There was only one thing for me to do.

I had to go shopping. In Maple Creek.

Did Maple Creek even have a clothing shop?

The Internet was no help. If there was a shop in Maple Creek, it didn't have a website. Didn't mean there wasn't one.

Just before ten, I headed out to walk downtown and find out.

I was in luck.

There was a little clothing store for women at the corner of Main Street and Jackson Blvd.

I stepped inside to the scent of lavender. The store window display suggested that they might have some summery clothes to choose from.

No one bothered me as I looked around. At least not at first.

I walked past the blue jeans and t-shirts. Not what I was looking for. I knew what I was looking for. I was looking for something that was casual and cool, but sophisticated.

A middle-aged woman came out from the back.

"Hello," she said. "I'm Sherry. Can I help you find something?"

"I need something. A dress, I think. Something cute, but professional."

"Cute, but professional."

Sherry put a finger on her chin. "What's the occasion?" she asked.

"A cookout."

"I might have something in the back," she said and disappeared again.

It always baffled me that people kept things in the back. How could they sell things if they weren't out for display?

While I waited, I browsed the racks of clothing. There were mostly things I would never wear. Long baggy pants. Tunics in bright colors. Not really my style. Looked more like something a grandmother would wear. Or maybe an expectant mother.

I wasn't feeling very hopeful when Sherry came back out, but she had something draped over her arm.

"I found just the thing," she said, smiling broadly.

"Great," I said, but still feeling doubtful.

Sherry held up a little pale green dress splashed with dark green flowers in a light soft-looking material.

"Oh," I said, holding out a hand to see if it was as soft as it looked. It was.

"Try it on," Sherry said, excitedly. "I just knew someone would come along that it would be perfect for."

"Okay," I said. Truly how could I not? I took the dress with me into the dressing room.

"You remind me of someone I used to know," Sherry said, talking to me through the curtain.

"Oh? Who's that?" I asked as I untied my canvas sneakers and slipped out of them.

"The girl who used to date Austin Devereaux." She paused a minute. "His mother used to come in here. Ava. You look like Ava."

With a sigh, I slid the dress over my head.

"I am Ava," I said.

"I knew it," Sherry said as I stepped out from behind the curtain. "Oh wow. That is just perfect. Come see."

She led me to a three-way mirror. I stepped into it and realized that she was absolutely right. The dress was perfect.

It was soft and airy, but not the least bit revealing. It had a high neckline and cap sleeves. Not too long or too short. It reached just below my knees and moved easily as I turned.

"I'll take it," I said, not even looking at the price tag. At this point I was not only desperate for an outfit to wear to the cookout, I was in love with this dress.

"It looks so good on you and it fits like it was made for you," she said.

The bell over the door rang, rescuing me from further comments.

"I'll be right back," she said.

I changed back into my clothes since I had a few hours before I needed to head out to the Devereaux's house.

By the time I was dressed again, Sherry waited for me behind the register.

"How long have you and Austin been married?" she asked.

"Married? We're not married."

"Oh. I could have sworn the two of you got married after you left here."

"Just one of those rumors, I guess."

"I guess." She folded the dress and placed it into a paper shopping bag. "I'm going to throw in these earrings," she said. "Just because they're perfect with this dress."

"You're very kind, Sherry," I said.

As I left her store, I mused that back home no one would ever think to throw in anything without charging for it.

That was something positive about living in a small town that I never would have realized if I hadn't moved to Houston.

Chapter Sixteen

AUSTIN

Lucky for her, my sister, Anastasia, had left for class by the time I got up the next morning.

But not before, however, she had done exactly what I was afraid she had done. She had sent a text to Ava from my phone inviting her over tonight.

I'd promised that I would invite her and I would have. But I would have done it on my terms. On my time.

I probably would have shown up at the inn and caught her off-guard. That was more my style. I liked the element of surprise.

My sister, however, believed in the straightforward, no holds barred approach.

But. She had saved me from having to wonder.

Ava had simply texted back one word. Okay.

My sister, with all her wonderful intentions, had left me in something of a quandary.

Anastasia wouldn't see it that way, of course. But she didn't know Ava like I did. The Ava that I knew would want to know what time she was supposed to be here. It wasn't like the old days when it was understood that we would just show up at one another's houses to do school work or just hang out. In Ava's case, school work was almost always involved.

She'd started taking college classes when we were juniors in high school. I could have done it, too, but I didn't much see the point.

Looking back, Ava and I would probably have stayed together if I had kept up with her pace academically.

I'd known I wanted to be a pilot, even back then, and I hadn't seen the point in rushing through the classes. So I hadn't. I'd waited until college to take college classes. As such, Ava and I never took a college class together.

My quandary was I could text her a time to be here. Or I could just show up to pick her up. Still. We needed to coordinate a time.

I'd already decided that I would pick her up. I decided that right out of the gate. Ava might live alone in the city of Houston, but I wasn't going to have her driving on these back roads alone. Not on my watch.

Since I hadn't been the one to text her about coming to begin with, it didn't seem right to tack on a time.

So I took a shower, put on a pair of blue jeans and a white shirt —all my shirts were white—and headed out to town.

On the way out, I walked past my dad, already meticulously cleaning the grill, getting it ready.

"A little hot, isn't it?" I asked. "To be out here?"

Father glanced up at the hot afternoon sun beating down on us. "I agree," he said. "but it has to be done. You headed to town to pick up Ava?"

Why was it everyone just assumed that I was back with Ava? Maybe it was the rumor—that I had started—that we were engaged. Still. My own family was quick to believe a rumor about me. Their own son.

Whatever it was, it wasn't something I could fight against.

"Yes," I said. "But whatever rumor you heard isn't true."

Father straightened and set the brush aside. His eyes twinkled with mischievousness.

"You mean about your engagement?"

"How could we be engaged?" I asked. "We just saw each other yesterday for the first time in over five years."

Father wiped his face with his sleeve.

"Sometimes time doesn't move in a linear fashion," he said.

"I don't even know what that means." Since Father seemed intent on having a serious conversation out here in the heat of the day, I moved over into the shade of a big maple tree about two yards away. It didn't help much, but it did help a little.

"It means," Father said, taking two bottles of water out of the cooler at his feet and coming to stand next to me. He handed me one of the wet bottles. "What that means is that love doesn't play by the rules. It doesn't care if five years have passed by or if you just saw her yesterday."

I twisted the top on my bottle of water, dried my hands on my jeans, and drank half of it. I couldn't disagree with him.

When I'd seen Ava sitting on the bench surrounded by green ivy tendrils, I'd essentially gone back in time. Time had folded back on itself and all my feelings were right there. Right on the surface again.

"When did you get so wise?" I asked my father.

He laughed. "I've always been wise. You just didn't know it."

"Good point. When is Jonathan getting here?"

Father glanced up again toward the sky. Jonathan would be flying in.

"He didn't say. But he'll be here."

"What's the occasion?" I asked. My oldest brother rarely came home without a reason.

"Didn't say."

"We'll find out soon enough, won't we?" I said. "I'm gonna get out of this heat and see if I can find Ava."

"Looking forward to seeing her again," Father said as I walked off.

My family had never said much to me about Ava. I'd gotten some pitying looks, but I'd figured I was projecting. Now I wasn't so sure.

Chapter Seventeen

AVA

I passed the afternoon by getting some work done. It was nice to work without being interrupted.

Taking a break, I called my neighbor, the closest thing I had to a best friend, and made sure she remembered to go over to feed Medley. My cat was going to be quite unhappy with me for being gone for two nights. Fortunately he liked my neighbor and she would spend some time with him. My neighbor didn't have the same work ethic I had. She was content to sit on the sofa and watch television for hours, Medley curled up in her lap.

By three o'clock, I started to get antsy.

I got into the shower, even though I'd already taken one that morning.

I took my time drying my hair, drying it straight with a little flip on the ends like my hair stylist had taught me.

The final effect wasn't as good as she could do, but it wasn't half bad considering. I even put on eyeshadow and mascara.

I figured going to a cookout with my high school boyfriend and his family counted as a special occasion.

After I put on the green dress, I automatically slipped into my heels.

Once trip across the room had me changing my mind. I slipped out of the heels and put on my white canvas sneakers.

A much better look. Relaxed and cute. That's what I was going for. Relaxed and cute with an air of professionalism.

I would just talk to Grandma Devereaux. Get a feel for where her head was. Then I would decide if I wanted to talk to her about selling her house.

It didn't seem right bringing it up at a family cookout and I wasn't going to do it. Ms. Miller had sent me here because I was good at what I did. Part of what made me good at what I did was my ability to read people and to time my interactions with them.

So that's what I was going to do.

I was going to time my interactions. If I didn't think she wanted to sell her home, then I wouldn't utter a word about it to her. Ms. Miller could do her own dirty work if she wanted to.

The Devereaux family was too important to me.

Dressed and ready to go, I put my crossbody bag over my shoulders and headed down to the lobby.

"Hey John," I said as I passed the desk.

"Hey Ava. There's someone here to see you."

"What? Who? Why didn't you call me?"

"I called. The volume's probably turned off on your phone. Nobody likes to be bothered by land lines anymore. Figured you were the same."

I didn't know if I was the same or not. To be honest, I didn't even know the room had a land line.

"Are they still here?" I asked.

When John nodded toward the front part of the lobby, I followed his gaze.

Austin stood up and walked toward me.

"You look beautiful," he said softly, for my ears only.

That was all I needed to hear to make the green dress worth it.

"Ready?" Without waiting for an answer, Austin took my hand and led me outside to his car.

If people didn't already believe we were engaged, it wouldn't take them long to decide that we were.

Chapter Eighteen

AUSTIN

I hadn't had to wait long for Ava at the inn. I'd had a short, but pleasant, conversation with John. John and I hadn't been friends in high school, but being in the same class in a small town gave us one of those unique bonds for life.

He and I talked about last night's football game. I hadn't been there, but I'd heard the highlights from my younger brother.

He rang Ava's room, even though I hadn't asked for her. Apparently the rumor about our engagement had spread like wildfire. Either that or he had made assumptions based on our long high school dating history. It wasn't as far-fetched as it sounded considering that he knew she was staying here. Seriously, why else would I just happen to stop by the first time in well... ever.

I wasn't sure which one I liked better. Probably our history. I could understand that a lot better than a rumor running through the town about me and Ava. It was a little hard to believe that people would be that focused on us. If so, I could only imagine that there must be a dearth of things to talk about in Maple Creek.

I couldn't help but picture people picking up their old rotary dial phones and calling each other, one after the other. Maybe I watched a little too many *Andy Griffith* reruns.

But seeing Ava again made all that vanish into the realm of the inconsequential.

She looked stunningly cute in a little green dress and white sneakers. Her hair was down, flowing around her shoulders with that freshly blow-dried look. I had sisters. I knew these things.

My father was right. The meaning of time simply vanished.

I took her hand and led her out to my car. Actually it was my father's car. A new silver Mercedes sedan.

I opened up the passenger seat and she slid right inside, then I went around and got into the driver's seat. It was just like old times. Different car.

"How long were you waiting?" Ava asked as I buckled up.

"Not long." I pulled out of the parking lot and turned right onto the main road. "I didn't know John worked here."

"I know. Me either. He knew everything about political science. I guess he didn't do anything with it."

"I hate that for him," I said. "I always figured he'd go into politics."

"He should have," Ava said. "But I guess he's just one of the many people who never leave the small town."

"Not us," I said, reaching over and squeezing her hand.

She smiled and my heart did little flips.

Were we supposed to talk about what happened back then when we broke up? Or were we supposed to just let bygones be bygones? I didn't know the protocol for dating an ex-girlfriend.

"Thanks for inviting me," she said. It was... unexpected."

"Yeah, well." I stopped at a red light on Main Street and watched as a new mother pushed a baby carriage across the street in front of us. "I was a little surprised, too."

Ava lifted an eyebrow, but didn't comment further on that.

"What's the occasion?" she asked.

I laughed. Even Ava knew there had to be an occasion for my father to fire up the grill. "Jonathan is coming home."

"Oh. Well. That explains it. What's he doing these days?"

"Still flying overseas."

"That must be hard on him. Being away so much."

I turned down the road winding through pine trees that would eventually end up at my family's house.

"I don't think he minds. He lives in Dallas now."

"Married?"

"Hardly. No woman in her right mind would marry him."

"I don't know," she said. "with him being a pilot and all, I'd think women would be lined up at his door."

"Lots of women, sure. But none in their right minds."

I drove around the circle drive and parked in front of the door.

"Looks like he's already here," I said.

"How do you know?" she asked as she unhooked her seatbelt.

"That's Mary's car." I nodded toward a little Nissan Sentra that had seen better days. "She picks him up from the airport."

"I thought you said he didn't have a girlfriend," Ava said, her brows creased.

"Just a friend. But between you and me, I think she would like to be more. I'll come around."

I went around. Opened her door and held out a hand to help her out.

With her hand in mine, I was reluctant to let go. Closing her car door, I decided it was too soon to walk in holding her hand, especially since I had denied the very rumors that I had started about us being engaged.

We walked through the quiet house, straight through to the backdoor to where everyone was.

"There is a God," I said as I walked out into the misting system. I'd been dreading this cookout primarily because of the heat.

Grandma saw Ava first and came right over. Gave her a hug.

"It's so good to see you, Dear," she said.

"It's wonderful to see you Mrs. Devereaux," Ava said. "How are you?"

"A little older," she said. "But hopefully a little wiser."

"You don't look a day older than the last time I saw you."

"I always liked you," she said, taking Ava by the arm and leading her to sit at the little table beneath a big red umbrella. "What a lovely dress."

I just stood there, watching as my family took her into their fold like she and I had never been apart. Maybe my father was right.

My sister, too. Anastasia insisted it was my fault for letting her go. I was beginning to think she was right.

Chapter Nineteen

AVA

The Devereaux backyard hadn't changed much over the years. The barbecue grill might be a little bigger. A little shinier.

The clear blue water in the swimming pool glimmered in the waning sunlight reminding me of many lazy afternoons spent sitting in a chair in the shallow water, with my iPad open to one of my textbooks.

But the misting system was definitely new.

I was a little overwhelmed with how easily the Devereauxs enveloped me back into their fold.

It was true that I had felt like I was part of their family back in high school, but I always figured they blamed me for the breakup with Austin. It had, after all, been me. I was the one who had broken up with him.

Thinking back, he hadn't had much to say that day I had unceremoniously broken the news to him that we didn't need to date anymore. I think I had expected him to say more. He'd said something like "It's okay. I understand."

And that had quite simply been that.

I'd told myself it was for the best. Buried myself in my schoolwork and, head down, kept going.

During the day, I was able to keep thoughts of him at bay, but at night... At night when I was sleeping, I would dream about him.

The Devereaux family was still large. His parents—Mr. and Mrs. Devereaux. The older Mrs. Devereaux, aka Grandma. The five siblings. Grandpa Devereaux was missing, as I had known he would be, but still his absence bruised my heart.

Jonathan was the oldest of the siblings. Six years older than Austin, so I hadn't gotten to know him well.

After Austin came Anastasia. She was less than a year younger than Austin. Austin and Anastasia were close. They argued and teased each other relentlessly, but protected each other from everyone else with a fierceness that couldn't be broken.

The two youngest had been children at the time and I hardly recognized them now.

Austin stood with Jonathan and their father at the grill, all of them holding bottles of beer. Mr. Devereaux looked like a quintessential middle-aged man enjoying being with this family. I could picture him at football games, cheering on his son.

Jonathan was tallest. Tall and lean. He carried a seriousness about him that made him seem aloof, but by all accounts, he was quite personable.

Then there was Austin. Austin was tall and lean, as well. A

couple of inches shorter than his six-foot two-inch brother. Unlike Jonathan, Austin seemed to be amused by something. Whenever he got mad about something, he just walked away. Probably what had happened when I had broken up with him. He'd simply walked away to process it in his own way.

Right now, I honestly, couldn't say what had been wrong with me at the time.

Grandma Devereaux was telling me about how she was trying to figure out a way to keep Scottie.

"But it's probably a felony to steal a guide dog, isn't it?" she asked. Scottie was sitting at her feet. It was almost as though the two of them were of like mind.

"I think it's only a felony if you get caught," I said.

"I like the way you think," she said.

"But. Unfortunately. I think Austin is responsible for Scottie right now so it might get him in trouble."

"Oh well. We don't want to do that, do we?"

Austin must have heard his name. He looked over at me and smiled. I automatically smiled back and a bevy of butterflies let loose in my stomach.

Being back here with him and his family warmed my heart. I had the sense that this was where I belonged. I hadn't felt this way anywhere else before or since.

But I was afraid to let myself feel like I belonged here because in truth I didn't.

I was only here for the night, then tomorrow I would drive back to Houston and resume my job working at home. Austin would go back to flying airplanes.

And we wouldn't see each other anymore.

I had to keep my mind focused on why I was really here. I was here to find out if Grandma Devereaux—Mrs. Devereaux—was interested in selling her home in Houston and not just selling it, but selling it to an investment company that would most like knock it down to build a parking garage or a shopping center.

Anastasia, looking comfortable in shorts and a t-shirt came outside, gave me a hug, then sat down next to me.

"I'm glad you're here," she said.

"Me too. It was nice of you all to invite me."

She just smiled and patted Scottie on the head.

I was a little like Scottie, I mused. They had taken Scottie in, even though he was only here temporarily. Same with me. They had taken me in, knowing that I was only here temporarily.

"How long can you stay?" Anastasia asked. It was almost like she had read my mind.

"I have to leave tomorrow."

"Tomorrow? That's too soon."

"I'm just here for work," I said, amused and a little confused by her statement.

"You young people work too much," Grandma Devereaux said.

"I absolutely agree," I said. "Do you still have your home in Houston?"

I felt like a heel asking her something I already knew.

"I do," she said, then lowered her voice. "But I'm thinking about moving in here. I haven't told anyone yet."

"You don't like living in Houston anymore?"

"There's a lot more to do, but since... well... I don't get out and do anything much now. It's just me sitting there in my big old house when my family is here."

"I would think that would be rather lonely," I said.

"I wish I had more time to visit," Anastasia said, jumping into the conversation. "But school keeps me busy."

"As it should," Grandma Devereaux said. "Don't you go feeling guilty."

"I'm going to get something to drink," Anastasia said. "Want something?"

"That would be nice," I said and Grandma Devereaux agreed.

Anastasia took off.

"What are you thinking you'll do with your house?" I asked, keeping my voice low as to not give away her secret.

"Oh. I don't know. I have so many memories wrapped up in there. My husband and I built it ourselves, you know. We picked out every single thing down to the light switches and door knobs. And don't think we didn't update them over the years." Her voice was wistful, sad even, and her eyes misted. "But we did every bit of it together."

"I know. I'm so sorry."

"But life goes on, doesn't it?" she said. "Now. I want you to tell me about your engagement to my grandson."

Chapter Twenty

AUSTIN

Anastasia cornered me in the kitchen when Mother sent me in to get some vegetables out of the refrigerator she had already cut up for the grill.

"You're going to keep her this time, right?" Anastasia said.

I knew exactly what she was talking about.

"As I already explained, she's the one who broke up with me."

"I don't think she meant it," Anastasia said, looking out at where Ava sat with Grandma, their heads bent together in conversation.

"Well, it wasn't an accident."

"But it was a mistake," she said.

"What makes you think this?" I set the plate of vegetables on the island. Mother could wait while I heard what my sister had to say.

"I just know."

"You've got to give me more than that."

Anastasia sighed. "Boys can be so stupid. Don't you see the way she looks at you?"

Not really. I was too busy looking at her.

"I don't know."

"Don't let her go this time," Anastasia said, opening the refrigerator and pulling out a pitcher of lemonade. She got out three glasses, filled them with ice, and set it all on a tray.

"How is it you seem so certain?" I asked.

Anastasia just smiled with a little shrug. I pitied the man who would have the misfortune of falling in love with her. My sister was as headstrong as she was beautiful. And on top of that, she was smart. Studying psychology just helped her channel her already intuitive mind.

"I just call it like I see it," she said. And then there was growing up with three brothers. Succinct and to the point.

"Do you need help carrying that?" I asked.

"Looks like you've got your hands full," she said, nodding toward the platter of fresh vegetables on the counter. "Come on. Let's not keep them waiting any longer."

"Good idea."

I couldn't decide if my sister was brilliant or crazy. Maybe she was just a pain in the ass.

It was rather hard to decide at this point.

Either way, I wasn't going to dismiss her observations out of hand.

The real reason I wasn't going to just dismiss her ideas was that I agreed with her.

When we stepped outside in the surprisingly cool misty air, Ava looked up and our gazes met.

I could rule out Anastasia being crazy. She was right.

My whole family was right.

I had let Ava go too easily.

That had been a different time and place. I'd had a lot going on at the time. My grandfather had been sick. I'd been getting a lot of flying hours to get my pilot's license.

I'd been under a lot of pressure. My grandfather wanted to see me get my pilot's license. So I had pushed myself. I had spent as much time in the air as possible to get my hours.

Somewhere in there, Ava had broken up with me. I'd blamed on me working too hard. Focusing too much on flying and family. Those days all blurred together in retrospect.

Grandpa had been at the little ceremony the school had held when I'd gotten my pilot's license. He had been so proud of me and that had made it all worth it.

He had died three weeks later.

The pain of my breakup with Ava had paled in comparison with the grief I'd felt during that time.

I hadn't fought for her. I hadn't even questioned her. I honestly hadn't had the energy.

In retrospect, I probably should have talked to her. Told her what I was going through. But at the time I just couldn't do it.

So I'd let her go.

Not again. Not now. Things were different now.

Chapter Twenty-One

AVA

"We're not really engaged," I told Grandma Devereaux.

She just nodded.

The appetizing scent of hamburgers and hotdogs on the grill would have tempted me if I hadn't been a vegetarian for just over two years now.

It should have been hot sitting outside with the sun glaring down just as it sat poised to dip over the horizon, but the misting system kept everything cool.

I hadn't seen very many misting systems in Houston. Mostly out west in Las Vegas. Mr. Devereaux was ahead of his time.

"I can't help but wonder where the rumor started," Grandma mused.

I took a deep breath and drank from the bottle of water someone had pressed into my hands.

"Do you know Danielle Barker?" I asked.

"I don't think so. Should I?"

"She was in our class. In high school."

"I don't know her."

I was ridiculously pleased that Grandma Devereaux didn't know who Danielle was. That meant that Austin had never brought her home. If he had, his grandmother would have remembered.

"Well. I think Austin might have told her that he was engaged. Then when she saw us together, she jumped to conclusions that no one bothered to correct."

I didn't tell her that not only had no one corrected her, but that Austin had kissed me on the lips right in front of her.

So Danielle had done more than just jump to conclusions. She had been pushed right into the crazy idea that Austin and I were engaged.

When Austin stepped outside, behind his sister, both carrying trays, his gaze immediately found mine and I swallowed hard.

I was so in trouble.

Anastasia set a tray with a pitcher of lemonade on the table and handed both of us glasses before she sat back down next to me.

"The rumor might not be true," Grandma Devereaux pointed out. "But you're here."

"Yes," I said. "I am here."

This would have been one of those logical places for me to tell her the real reason why I was in Maple Creek.

Another one of those turning points. But I couldn't bring myself to do it. I'd known this ahead of time. I'd known that this was a social visit and I had no intention coming here to tell her that I'd originally been sent here for work.

The truth was, I was no longer here for work, if I ever was.

The moment I'd seen Austin, work had become secondary.

I thought about Ms. Miller. Wondered why she hadn't tried to get in touch with me. She was far too hands-on to let me go alone on this deal without at least checking in.

I sipped the cold lemonade and settled into the moment.

For this moment in time, however short it might be, all was right with my world.

Things only got better when Austin came to our table after he dropped off his own tray.

"Trade places with me," he said to his sister.

Anastasia promptly slid out of her chair and I didn't miss the look that passed between brother and sister. I couldn't interpret the look, but I knew it was one of those brother sister looks that said something that only they would understand.

But with Austin sitting shoulder to shoulder with me, my thoughts shifted to pure emotion.

He smelled good. Like wood smoke from the grill blended with whatever masculine scented soap he used.

He smiled at me.

"What are you girls doing over here?"

Grandma Devereaux made a face and leaned close.

"He's just like his grandfather," she said.

"In what way?" I asked. I really wanted to know what she saw in Austin that reminded her of Austin's grandfather.

"Always had a smile and something charming to say."

Since he had only asked what we were doing, I didn't quite make the connection.

But Grandma Devereaux would know better than anyone.

"Are you suggesting I should be wary of him?" I asked, knowing full well that Austin could hear every word.

"Not you, Dear. You're the one who will keep him straight."

"I'm right here," Austin said.

"He knows what I'm talking about," Grandma Devereaux said.

"I'm gonna go talk to Jonathan," Anastasia said, standing up, then stopped. "Where's Mary?"

"She had something she had to do," Austin said. "I'm sure she'll be back."

I was curious about this thing with Jonathan and Mary, but it didn't seem to be any of my business.

"Maybe not," Anastasia said to herself as she walked toward her oldest brother.

I looked at Austin, but he just shrugged and drank from his beer bottle.

"Is someone going to tell me what this Danielle Barker has to do with the rumor about you two?"

Austin and I looked at each other.

"I don't think she has anything to do with anything," Austin said.

"See," Grandma Devereaux said. "A charmer."

Finding it entertaining that Grandma saw things in Austin I didn't, I just smiled and enjoyed the feeling of being swept up into the family had missed terribly.

Chapter Twenty-Two

AUSTIN

There were a lot of family dynamics going on right now that I needed to explore further.

One of them was my grandmother and the possibility that she might be moving in here. It begged the question about what she would do with her house. It was practically a mansion right there in downtown Houston, tucked in between the high rises, securely and barely noticeable.

The other curiosity was my brother Jonathan. I still didn't know what kind of occasion had brought him home. Furthermore, his friend Mary always stayed for dinner. But not tonight. Something was different.

And Jonathan, being serious as he was, was hard to read. I

couldn't tell if anything was bothering him or not. He looked and acted the way he always did. Aloof and unconcerned.

Sometimes I wished I could be more like Jonathan. Problems seemed to simply roll off his back like water on a duck's feathers. At the same time, I felt like maybe he was missing out on life experiences that had nothing to do with airplanes.

I didn't hold his love of airplanes against him. I was just as bad about that.

But. I'd had a girlfriend—Ava—and that had trumped everything else, even if it had ended badly between us.

It hadn't ended so badly though that we couldn't have a second chance. That was important. I knew couples that had ended so badly they couldn't be in the same room with each other.

Instead, I was having trouble focusing on much of anything other than Ava sitting next to me, looking pretty and fresh and as lovely as she had all those years ago when I had loved her.

I had loved her and I still loved her. My family loved her.

In fact, my own family blamed me for *her* breaking up with me when I hadn't done anything. Of course, for them that was the whole problem.

I'd managed to not blame myself over the years. Unfortunately, I wasn't doing so well at not blaming myself right now.

Fortunately, I was a look forward to the future kind of guy. So that's what I was going to do. I was going to look forward to the future.

I was not going to dwell on the past. Bygones were bygones and as far as I was concerned, Ava was brand new.

She felt brand new.

When I'd kissed her, it had felt like a first kiss, even though it wasn't.

It had felt more like going home.

They said a person couldn't go home again. I had to disagree on that.

I was home again.

With my family and with Ava.

Even more important, they all got along with each other. As far as we were concerned, Ava was already part of the family, even if she didn't know it.

"I need to take Scottie for a walk," I said to no one in particular.

When no one answered, I turned to Ava.

"Do you want to come with me?" I asked her.

Grandma nudged her. "I'll see you in a little bit."

Ah. What the hell.

I held out a hand and Ava took it.

Walking hand in hand, we walked out toward the swimming pool.

And just like that, we circled back around again.

Chapter Twenty-Three

AVA

Austin and I walked along the path that led to the Devereauxs' in-ground pool. It wasn't a big pool, just big enough for splashing around and staying cool on a summer day. Big enough for five lounge chairs on the shallow end.

The opposite side had a pile of well-placed rocks meant to look like they just naturally landed there. A perpetual waterfall tumbled over those rocks creating an especially peaceful setting this time of day between the setting sun and the moon glow.

As we walked around the pool toward a bench, Austin still held my hand.

It felt both natural and new. My blood rushed through my veins, making my knees a little weak as we sat down side by side.

He clasped my hand tightly in his, resting our clasped hands on his thigh.

I didn't want to think too much. I didn't want to think about how tomorrow we would go back to our normal lives.

"Look," I said. "Lightning bugs."

"We don't see those in the city," he said.

"No." I leaned back against the wooden bench. "Do you ever wish you had stayed here or maybe came back here?"

"That's a complicated question," he said.

"Really? I thought it would be a hard no."

He looked across the pool where his family was gathered for the cookout.

"I miss my family sometimes," he said.

"I'm sorry about your grandfather."

"Yeah," he said, running a hand over his face. "Me too."

We sat in silence for a few minutes watching the lightning bugs. Listening to the waterfall and the occasional laughter from his family.

"I should have told you," he said.

"You should have told me what?"

"I should have told you that he was sick."

"Who? Your grandpa?"

"He was already sick when... before we broke up."

"Austin." I put my other hand on his, imagining the pain that he must be feeling by telling me this. "Why didn't you tell me?"

He turned and looked into my eyes. His blue eyes shining brightly.

"I couldn't," he said. "As long as I didn't tell you, it didn't quite seem real."

"I'm so sorry," I said and put my arms around him, resting my cheek against his chest.

He put his arms around me and rested his chin on the top of my head.

I sighed and thought about how right it felt to be here with him.

If I could turn back the hands of time, I would change whatever it took to take me back to the time before I decided breaking up with Austin was the right thing to do.

It had been a mistake. I had been so obsessively focused on getting my master's degree and getting a good career.

But now that I had those things—the master's degree and the good job—I would give it all up to have a life with Austin.

It was too late now. Too late to go back and change what I had done.

Life had gone on.

Austin had gone on.

Fate had given us this moment and I never wanted it to end.

Chapter Twenty-Four

AUSTIN

The gentle flow of water falling over the rocks into the swimming pool was soothing.

I had grown up here. I had so many memories from right here in my parents' backyard. I considered myself a city boy now. I flew airplanes all over the country. I had my own place in the city—a place I considered my home.

And yet right now, I felt like I belonged here in Maple Creek.

It was rather disconcerting.

I didn't belong in Maple Creek, exactly. I had family here and it was a good place to have grown up.

But even though I didn't belong in Maple Creek, I did belong with Ava.

Sitting here on the wooden bench with her, a bench my father had built my mother before they had Jonathan, I knew I belonged with Ava.

My parents liked to talk about how they built this bench before they decided to build a swimming pool. They talked about building a swimming pool for several years before they did it. I was a teenager before they broke ground on it.

Starting out, they were just going to make a waterfall with a little pool, but that didn't make sense to them. As the parents of five children, they realized that a swimming pool was actually quite logical.

They had been right.

Ava and I had sat out here in these pool chairs often over the long summers. I tended to nap in the sunshine, but she wore a broad brimmed hat and used the time to read her textbooks.

I should have noticed just how far ahead of me she was getting in school.

That wouldn't have mattered though if she and I had talked more. I didn't tell her about what was going on with my grandfather and she didn't tell me what I was doing that made her think we shouldn't be together.

And like my sister said, I hadn't fought for her. I should have fought for her. I could have so easily turned things around.

We had wasted all those years apart. Years we could have spent together. We could have children of our own by now.

But looking back at life's decisions was a lot like being an armchair quarterback. It was easy to look back and see what should have been done.

In the moment, however, things looked different. In the moment, down in the weeds, it was hard to make the right choice. It was hard to even see what the right choice was.

In the moment, maybe there wasn't a right choice. There were just choices.

If we hadn't broken up, she might not have the career she had and I might not have the career I had. Would we have been tempted to stay in Maple Creek or would we would have braved the world together?

I had a feeling she and I would have found our way to Houston together if not separately.

Together would have been a whole lot more fun.

"You seem deep in thought," Ava said.

"I was just thinking."

Straightening, she looked at me sideways, her brows furrowed.

"I was thinking about how we used to spend our afternoons out here."

"You napped."

"And you studied," I said with a grin.

"It was nice," she said.

"We were good together."

She looked into my eyes, searching. Even in the low light, her mysterious green eyes enchanted me like sunlight dancing in a grassy meadow.

Her lips parted slightly and confusion flittered across her features.

I wasn't confused. I knew what I wanted.

I wanted what I had wanted all along.

I wanted Ava.

Leaning forward, my lips hovering close to hers, I felt her breath hitch just a little.

I lightly pressed my lips against hers, letting the memory of kissing her blend in with the newness of kissing her. It was rather intoxicating.

Pressing my palms against her cheeks, I lifted my head just enough to see that her eyes were closed. That was invitation enough.

Beneath the soft glow of moonlight and the gentle flow of the waterfall, I kissed her again.

Chapter Twenty-Five

AVA

We made it back in time to eat with the rest of Austin's family.

Austin ate a hamburger while I ate grilled vegetables.

I sat at one of the outside picnic tables between Austin and his grandmother.

"Are you sure you've got enough to eat, Dear?" Grandma Devereaux asked, noticing that I only ate vegetables.

"This is actually more than I usually eat," I said.

"She always did forget to eat," Austin said.

I smiled at him and he smiled back.

I felt like I had stars in my eyes. I couldn't stop smiling. Austin hadn't left my side since we'd kissed on the other side of the swimming pool.

If anyone else knew, they didn't say anything and on the other hand, no one seemed to be the least bit surprised that we seemed to be together.

I didn't know if Austin's mother and grandmother really were already planning our wedding, but it was quite possible.

"You always made sure I did, though," I told him.

Grandma Devereaux leaned over so only I could hear.

"It's what the Devereaux men do," she said. "They take care of their women."

A lot of girls would have insisted that they didn't need to be taken care of by a man and would have told her so.

But I found it all quite charming. I found it charming that she told me that and I found it sweet that he would do it. As to my way of thinking, there was nothing wrong with having a man around to remind a girl to eat.

Nothing at all.

It would certainly be hard to complain when that guy was the handsome Austin Devereaux.

A girl would be crazy to complain about that.

"It's what any guy would do," Austin said, obviously listening in on my conversation with his grandmother.

I let their subsequent banter drift into the background. It might sound like something any guy would do, but it wasn't.

I hadn't dated a lot, but I'd dated enough to know that most guys were only interested in taking care of themselves. If a girl wanted to come along, they were okay with it. If she didn't then that was her loss.

Austin was his own man, but he had always been good about putting my needs first.

That was rare.

And now that I thought about it, I realized I had always compared other guys to Austin.

No one else had ever stood a chance.

"You have to come over tomorrow," Anastasia said.

At first I didn't realize she was talking to me.

"Okay," I said. "What's the occasion?"

"There's no occasion, but it's Sunday," she said. "You shouldn't have to stay at the inn by yourself. Right Austin?"

"That is true."

"I was planning on driving back tomorrow," I said. I'd been planning it, even though I hadn't done what I had set out to do here in Maple Creek.

"At least come for lunch," Grandma Devereaux said. "We always have a big lunch on Sunday."

"I remember," I said, glancing over at Austin. He gave me a little nod. "Okay," I said. "I can do that."

"Good," Anastasia said. "Since you're coming, I'll bake a dessert. Do you have a preference?"

"I'm sure that whatever you make will be wonderful."

"If she ever decides to drop out of psychology, she could open a bakery," Grandma Devereaux said.

Anastasia wrinkled her nose. "Let's not get carried away, Grandma. If I had to do it all the time, I wouldn't like it anymore."

"I don't know. Austin flies all the time and he never gets tired of it, do you Austin?"

"Not really."

"And Ava." Grandma Devereaux put a hand over mind. "I'm sorry. I don't know what you do."

I gulped down a swallow of water as the table seemed to go silent, waiting for me to answer.

"I work for an investment company," I said.

"Do you ever get tired of it? Grandma Devereaux asked.

"Actually sometimes I do."

That had the desired effect. It made everyone laugh and it got the spotlight off of me as they went on to the next topic which had something to do with Anastasia and her becoming a psychologist.

I was content to just sit here with Austin's shoulder touching mine.

I was sinking fast, but I'd worry about what to do about it tomorrow.

Maybe the next day.

Chapter Twenty-Six

AUSTIN

If I could freeze time, now would be one of those rare moments that I would choose to do so.

I sat next to Ava at one of the picnic tables while my family sat around talking about nothing in particular.

Grandma seemed happier than I had seen her since Grandpa got sick.

That in itself was enough to make this a good day.

And then having Ava here with me made the day all that much better.

I had some things to figure out, but I knew I wasn't going to figure them out tonight.

At ten-thirty Grandma announced that it was past her bedtime. Mother and Father agreed and everyone began to scatter.

"Ready to go back to the inn?" I asked Ava.

"Sure," she said, without any noticeable enthusiasm.

We didn't talk on the short drive back to the inn.

I walked her inside, past John who sat behind the desk, phone pressed to his ear, to the elevator.

"You don't have to go up," she said.

"I'll make sure you get to your door," I said. "Can't have it getting back to Grandma that I wasn't a gentleman."

"That wouldn't be good, would it?"

I stepped into the elevator behind her and after riding up to her floor, we walked down the hallway toward her door.

"I'm glad you came today," I said as we reached her door.

"Me too." She turned and looked into my eyes.

"My grandmother especially enjoyed seeing you."

"She's a lovely lady."

"I'll pick you up in the morning," I said.

"I'll be ready." She took a step back, stopping with her back against the door.

I put my right hand on the door casing behind her and cupped her cheek with my left palm. Her eyes drifted closed and her red bow-shaped lips parted.

I leaned forward, pressed a kiss against the corner of her lips.

She sighed.

I kissed one eyelid, then the other.

"I missed you," I said before I pressed my lips against hers.

She ran her fingers through hair that barely brushed my collar, holding onto me.

I don't know how long we stood there, neither of us able to get close enough to the other.

I could have stood there all night, just kissing her, but the elevator doors opened, and being ever cognizant of how quickly gossip spread in Maple Creek, I quite reluctantly released her.

Even though the man walked in the other direction, I stood so that I shielded her from being seen.

She pulled her key out of her purse and slid it into the door lock. The old inn had been upgraded in some ways, but the original door locks had never been changed to electronic. It was part of the old inn's charm.

"Good night," she said, turning the door knob and stepping inside.

"Good night, Little One" I said just as she closed the door.

I stood there and waited until I heard her turn the deadbolt.

The only thing that kept me from knocking on her door was knowing that I would see her again in the morning.

I had to let her sleep.

It was, after all, part of my job to take care of her.

Chapter Twenty-Seven

AVA

After locking the door, I leaned against it with weak knees.

Austin was so unexpected.

I pressed my fingers against my swollen lips. I hadn't been so thoroughly and completely kissed since... well... since I was with Austin.

It had been so very easy to fall back in love with him.

And I had.

It wasn't, of course, like I had ever stopped loving him.

My feelings had just been tucked away, left to simmer in the background.

Kissing him, no actually just seeing him, had fanned all those feelings back to life.

I pushed off the door and went through my nightly routine.

I put my phone on charge. Still no messages. Very strange.

Changed into my sleep shorts and a Houston Astros t-shirt.

Washed my face and brushed my hair.

I replayed Austin's kisses over and over.

I didn't know what I was going to do about him.

His family had invited me back tomorrow for Sunday lunch. I had to go, of course. What's more, I wanted to go.

I cherished being pulled back into his family's fold. It was overwhelmingly pleasantly unexpected.

Maybe I had been hasty in thinking that nothing could come of my renewed relationship with Austin.

We did, after all, both live in Houston.

To think that he'd lived there all along and I hadn't even known it.

To say that Houston was a big place was an understatement.

But we lived in the same city.

That was something.

Maybe it was everything.

I sat on the edge of the bed and stared outside at the full moon.

I had an appreciation now for Maple Creek that I hadn't had before. Growing up here, my main focus had been on getting out. I wanted to get away from here and never planned on coming back.

But now. Now I had Austin again.

And for the first time in a very long time I felt hopeful.

Hopeful that Austin and I could pick up where we left off. Or if not pick up where we left off, maybe we could put the past behind us and forge something new.

If his kisses were any indication at all, then it was very possible.

It was very possible that we could build onto our past and maybe this time make something that would last.

Maybe we could have what his grandparents had. A love that lasted through the ages. We might not live in Maple Creek, but wherever we lived we could still have that forever love.

But I was getting ahead of myself.

I had to remember why I was in Maple Creek.

Austin had called me *Little One.* He had called me *Little One* when we were dating. The only person who had ever, before or since, called me that.

Gazing out the window at the wispy clouds drifting across the full moon, I decided right then and there that I was not going to be the one to ask Grandma Devereaux about selling her home.

Someone else could do it.

Ms. Miller might ban me from working from home behind it, but I was not going to compromise what I believed in.

Just because I hadn't grown up with a strong family, or maybe because I hadn't, I believed in family. And if Austin's family could be my family, then I would pick that over my job any day of the week.

If Ms. Miller was especially nasty to me, I would resign and go out on my own. I'd been thinking about doing that anyway. I had my own way of working that didn't always match up with what was expected by an organization.

Austin was what mattered to me.

I'd always known it, but now it was front and center in my head.

I knew now what was important.

Chapter Twenty-Eight

AUSTIN

I drove home beneath the light of a full moon.

Tomorrow I would talk to Ava about Houston.

Bottom line. I wanted to be her boyfriend again.

And the beauty of it was that we already knew each other well enough that we didn't have to have a long engagement.

After I let myself in through the back door, I found Anastasia curled up in the living room reading a book.

"So," she said. "When's the wedding?"

"You're jumping on that bandwagon, too?" I asked, even though I had just been thinking the exact same thing. I certainly wasn't going to admit it to Anastasia.

"Hard not to when you're wearing that goofy expression." Anastasia rolled her eyes.

"I don't know what you're talking about." I sat down across from her. "What are you reading?"

"Oh no," she said, hugging the book against her. "You aren't going to change the subject."

"You want to talk about Ava?" I asked with a mischievous grin.

"We all like her and you know it," Anastasia said with a hint of indignation.

I leaned back and crossed an ankle over my other knee.

"I like her, too," I said, serious now.

"So what are you going to do about it?"

"I guess first of all, thanks to you, I'll bring her to lunch tomorrow."

"You're welcome."

I laughed. "I haven't forgotten that you're the one who got her here tonight. So... what is it you want in return?"

"I'll think of something. In the meantime, you'll just have to owe me."

"As far as younger sisters go, you have an evil streak."

Anastasia laughed and opened her book. "Get some sleep. You have to be up early tomorrow."

"Don't you?"

"I'll be okay," she said with a dismissive wave of the hand.

Knowing that she would, I went upstairs to my bedroom.

My sister was right about the goofy grin on my face. I couldn't wipe it away if I wanted to.

I hummed to myself as I got ready for bed. Scottie pushed my bedroom door open and came into my room. Ignoring my warning glance, he jumped onto my bed.

"Yeah," I said, pulling off one shoe, then the other. "Don't get too comfortable."

He barked once, then circled around three times before lying down, his head on his front paws.

I was going to miss him. Maybe Ava and I would get a dog.

Crazy. I was thinking crazy thoughts. Jumping way ahead of the game. I couldn't help it. It was the way my mind worked.

I didn't do baby steps anything, at least not when I set my mind to something.

I realized with a start that I had set my mind to Ava.

She and I had a lot of logistics to figure out, but she lived in Houston, for God's sakes. How hard could it be for us to have a normal relationship?

For all I knew, we could even live in the same zip code.

I would most definitely find out tomorrow. Before she left. If she hadn't driven, I would have flown her back to Houston. Not that it was that far. Just that it would allow us to spend more time together.

We would have plenty of time, I decided.

I had to take my time and court her properly.

Taking my time was going to be hard to do with all the women in my family already planning the wedding.

There was one thing about my family. We were rarely wrong about each other. I might not could see what was going on with me, but if I looked to my family, they could see it.

It was not a hardship to listen to them when it came to Ava. I was right there with them.

Tomorrow. Tomorrow I would let her know how I felt. That I wanted to keep seeing her.

Before getting into bed, I opened my shades and let the moonlight in.

It was a full moon. Anything could happen.

Chapter Twenty-Nine

AVA

"You seriously made this from scratch?" I asked Anastasia as I tossed the little wooden spoon she'd handed me in the trash.

"It's not a big deal," she said, shrugging off the compliment.

Making German chocolate frosting from scratch seemed like a big deal to me. I wouldn't even know where to start.

Austin sat on one of the bar stools at the kitchen island, watching us. Everyone else was in the living room watching some kind of football program. Apparently there was a big game starting soon.

We'd had dinner and everyone had pitched in to help clean up. Now Anastasia was making one of her famous desserts.

"Well," Anastasia said. "You can't leave until after we have cake."

I sat down next to Austin.

"I think your family is plotting against me," I said. "To get me to stay all day."

"Would that be so bad?" he asked, sweeping a strand of hair behind my ear.

"Maybe not," I said with a little shrug. "I do have to go to work tomorrow."

"I thought you were here for work," he said.

"I was, but... Let's not talk about work."

"Okay."

Someone yelled at the television followed by laughter.

"Did you find out why Jonathan is here?"

"No. I think he just wanted to come home."

"Hmm."

The doorbell rang. Scottie sat up and barked three times.

"I don't think Scottie likes visitors," I said.

"Probably not. He knows he has to leave soon and I think he's worried about someone coming to get him."

"That's sad," I said. "I hate to see him go."

"We all do," Austin said. "But he has work to do."

"He's a good dog," I said, scratching him behind the ears.

"Okay," Anastasia said, wiping her hands on her apron before slipping it off. "Now we just wait for the cake to cool so I can put the icing on it."

Someone turned the television off and I froze at the sound of a familiar voice.

"I must be hallucinating," I said to myself.

"Why do you say that?" Austin asked.

"For just a minute, I thought I heard my boss's voice."

"That would be very odd," Austin said.

"You're not kidding."

"Yeah. Well. Let's go see."

"You two go ahead. I'm staying here," Anastasia said.

With a foreboding feeling, I followed Austin into the living room.

And there was Ms. Miller. Sitting there in one of the Devereaux's oversized chairs. She sat on the edge, almost like she wasn't planning on sitting there for very long or maybe she was too good to actually sit down in one of their chairs.

I saw the surprise and maybe a bit of satisfaction when she looked over and saw me.

"It's her," I said, putting a hand on Austin's arm. "My boss. Ms. Miller."

"Hello Ava," Ms. Miller said.

"Why are you here?" I asked.

"We were just having a little discussion," Ms. Miller said.

"A discussion?" I felt a little weak in the knees. Fortunately, I was still holding onto Austin's arm.

I glanced around at the other Devereauxs in the room. Everyone had left except for Mr. and Mrs. Devereaux and Grandma Devereaux.

They all looked at me with what I could only call consternation. Consternation and confusion.

"Come," Ms. Miller said. "Join us. You're part of this conversation, after all."

Somehow, I'm not sure how—maybe I just followed Austin—I ended up sitting on the sofa next to Austin on one side and Grandma Devereaux on the other across from the others.

Why wasn't anyone saying anything? They were all just looking at me.

"As I was saying," Ms. Miller said. "Ava is here for work. She told you, right?"

The Devereauxs nodded, looking from me to Ms. Miller.

"Did she tell you what that job is?"

"She's an investor," Grandma Devereaux said, coming to my rescue.

"Never mind," Ms. Miller said. "Let me clarify."

I was going to be sick.

Why was this happening? How was this happening?

I pressed my fingers against my eyes. I must be in the middle of a bad nightmare.

"As I was saying," Ms. Miller said. "The reason she's here is to convince Mrs. Devereaux." She nodded toward Grandma Devereaux. "To sell the Sterling property in Houston. That was her only task."

I was shaking my head. No. I didn't want them to believe Ms. Miller. Yes. That was why she had sent me here, but that wasn't the reason I was here.

But they were all looking at me. Accusing. I saw accusation on their faces. I couldn't even bring myself to look at Austin.

I needed to go. I was going to be sick.

Jumping up, I raced out of the room, back to the kitchen and into the bathroom.

"Are you okay?" Anastasia asked.

"No." I opened the bathroom door, but stopped.

I didn't need to be here.

"Anastasia," I said. "Take me home. Please. Take me back to the inn."

"But what about Austin?"

"No," I said. "I can't. Just drive me back."

When she didn't move, I went toward the door.

"Where are you going?"

"I'm going to walk back. To the inn."

"No," Anastasia said. "You can't walk. It's too far." She came around the counter. Picked up a set of keys.

They were still talking in the other room. Mostly Ms. Miller was talking. I heard her voice, deceptively calm and congenial. They didn't know her. They didn't know she was a snake in the grass. Even *I* hadn't known the woman had this in her.

"Come on," Anastasia said. "I'll drive you."

"Thank you," I said, tears of gratitude clouding my eyes. "Thank you so much."

All I could think about as I followed her outside to her car was that I needed to get away from here.

Everything was falling apart.

Everything with Austin. With his family.

Destroyed.

I was vaguely aware that Anastasia tried to talk to me on the drive back. I didn't answer her. I couldn't. I just stared straight ahead. Counting the minutes until I could be in my own car.

I was already packed and checked out. Ready to go. I just needed to get to my car.

"Right here," I said, looking over at her as she pulled up in front of the Maple Creek Inn. "Thank you, Anastasia. I'm eternally grateful."

"Tell me what happened."

I shook my head. I'd already said all the words I could get past the lump in my throat.

I pushed the door open, but I before I stepped out of Anastasia's car, I looked back at her.

"It's not true," I said.

"What's not true?" she asked. "Tell me. Please."

"I'm sorry."

Then I stepped out of the car and hurried toward my own car in the lot at the side of the inn.

I sat in my car, the air conditioner blowing cold air in my face, until I saw Anastasia drive off.

It was over.

I backed out of the parking space and headed south toward Houston.

I had believed.

But I had believed in an illusion.

Chapter Thirty

AUSTIN

I sat in the living room of my parents' house and listened to someone named Clara Miller talk about how Ava was here to get Grandma to sell her property. The Sterling House in Houston.

The Sterling House was the home Grandma and Grandpa had built together. It was still her home.

According to Clara Miller, it was in a prime location for investors.

When I asked her what investors, she only had vague answers such as a company interested in building a high-rise condo building. Or another company interested in building a parking garage for the downtown tunnel system.

I knew exactly where my grandmother's house was. I knew that it was in a prime location for any number of things.

But this woman sounded full of bullshit to me. She sounded like she was making things up as she went. Saying things would make it seem like we had no choice but to sell my grandmother's home. Surely she didn't think because my family lived in a small town, they were ignorant. Didn't she know that my grandmother lived in Houston? She lived in Sterling House.

When I saw Anastasia's car pass by the front of the house, I went to the kitchen to look for Ava. She wasn't there.

Had Anastasia taken her somewhere?

There was only one way to find out.

Unfortunately, I spent the next fifteen minutes searching for my cell phone.

When I finally found it, I dialed my sister's phone number first. Following the questionable ringtone she had chosen for me—I'd ask her about that later—I found her phone in the kitchen.

She'd driven off without it.

My sister never went anywhere without her cell phone.

My mind immediately conjured a thousand emergencies that had my sister racing toward the ER with Ava.

My hands shaking, I dialed Ava's number. Straight to voicemail.

What the—?

I went back to the door where my grandmother was obviously finished listening to Clara Miller.

As I watched, she stood up, stretching herself to her full height of five three and stared down at the taller Clara Miller.

"You need to leave now," Grandma said.

Clara Miller stood up. Reached into a leather portfolio she wore on her shoulder.

"Of course," she said with an obviously fake smile. "But I'd like to leave this offer with you. I think you'll find it to be considerable."

How was it possible that this woman, this Clara Miller, dared to look down her nose at my grandmother?

I clenched my fists at my sides as my protective instincts toward my family kicked in. This woman had no right to come in here like this. To talk about Ava the way she had.

Grandma ignored the papers Clara Miller held out to her.

The woman just shrugged and laid them down on the coffee table.

Calm now, but full of purpose, I strode forward, picked up the papers, thrust them back into the woman's hands and, making sure not to lay a finger on her, held out my arm in an invitation for her to go to the door.

With a little shrug that made me want to smack her—and I would have if she'd been a man—I got her through the door and slammed it behind her.

"Don't come back," I said to her through the door.

My parents and grandmother sat there, looking stunned.

"What was that all about?" I asked.

Father was the first one to speak.

"Ava works for Clara Miller," he said. "Ava was sent here to get us to sell the Sterling Property to investors."

"She tricked us," Mother said, shaking her head.

I looked at my grandmother. "Did Ava say anything to you about the Sterling Property?"

"Not a word," she said, putting her hands on her hips.

"She wasn't here for that," I said.

"Clara said that it was her whole purpose for being in Maple Creek," Father said.

"Clara said a lot of things," Grandma said, her jaw clenched. "I don't believe any of it."

She handed me the woman's business card she seemed to suddenly remember she held in her hand.

"I'm going to lie down."

"Ava lied to us," Mother said after Grandma was out of earshot.

"She didn't lie," I said. "We know Ava. Are you choosing the words of that stranger, that Clara Miller woman, over someone you've known for over ten years?"

"I don't know," Mother said looking to Father.

Disgusted with my parents, I left as my grandmother had, but I wasn't going to take a nap. I was going to find Ava.

Chapter Thirty-One

AVA

One Week Later

I adjusted my skirt and straightened my jacket that didn't need straightening.

I shouldn't be nervous, but I was. Unlike Medley stretched out on my bed, idly licking his paws.

"Does this look okay?" I asked him.

He stopped licking his paws long enough to look at me, but just blinked and licked his paw again before using it to wash his ear.

Apparently I was disturbing his bath time.

In about an hour, I had my first meeting with my first investment client.

I'd reserved the conference room on the first floor for our meeting. I had my proposal professionally prepared and printed. I had my new business cards.

I had named my company *Maple Street Brokers.*

Maple was a nod to the nostalgia I had acquired for Maple Creek. I couldn't bring myself to name it Maple Creek Brokers. I didn't want my new company to be confused with a small-town firm.

"Okay," said to Medley. "You wait here. I shouldn't be long."

Medley rolled over and stretched.

At the risk of getting cat hair on my suit, I ran my hand along his fur.

I'd been working toward this moment since the day Clara Miller had shown up at the Devereaux family's home and turned my world upside down.

On the drive back to Houston, I had made my decision. It had been one of the easiest important decisions I had ever made.

I could not work for that woman anymore. I wouldn't do it.

Fortunately, since I worked at home, I had no reason to go by the office. No personal items to bring home. I'd already done that.

In retrospect, I wondered if maybe I had unconsciously been moving in this direction when I'd decided to work from home.

Stepping onto the elevator, I shored up my confidence. I was good at what I did and I was prepared.

An hour later, I had signed my first deal.

Going back up the elevator to my condo, it occurred to me that I had no one to celebrate with. No coworkers to go to lunch with.

Even my neighbor, who might would have gone to lunch with me to celebrate was out of town.

I was alone.

Back in my apartment, I dropped my keys and portfolio on the kitchen table and stepped out of my heels. Heels that my feet had quickly become unaccustomed to.

Then I checked my phone.

No calls.

For the first few days after I'd left Maple Creek, Austin had called me at least once a day. Then the calls had stopped.

I never answered.

I couldn't stand the thought of him yelling at me or worse telling me how disappointed in me he was for coming up to Maple Creek under the guise of befriending him and his family so I could make a sale.

It was far from the truth, but not far enough. Not nearly far enough.

So he stopped calling.

I thought about calling him. Explaining. But I didn't have the heart.

It was easier and cleaner to just jerk the band aid off. Less painful in the long run.

Chapter Thirty-Two

Austin

It took some doing, but I located Ava. It would have been so much easier if she had just answered her phone.

I didn't text her. I could have texted her, but I didn't want get into a texting conversation. I wanted to talk to her, but mostly I wanted to *see* her.

Since Grandma had given me her card, I had started with Clara Miller, but that had been a dead end. Ava had quit immediately. I took heart from that. It reinforced my belief in her. I knew that Ava had not come to my family under false pretenses.

I *knew* her. For one thing, I knew that her kisses were real.

If Clara Miller had sent her to talk to my grandmother, and I didn't doubt that she did, Ava had not followed through. My best guess was that she had decided not to bring it up after I'd invited her to my home socially and she and I had begun to get reacquainted.

I believed that with all my heart.

Then I'd had to work. I had four flights that kept me in the air most of the week. One of those flights was getting Scottie back to Birmingham.

I didn't know what happened and it wasn't my business to ask. I didn't know if Scottie's new owner had changed her mind or if something had happened or just why Scottie had to be return to the training facility.

What I did know was that when I dropped Scottie off and handed him off to the tech, Scottie had started howling.

I'd never heard him howl before. I went back, knelt in front of him, and the dog licked my face.

Needless to say, it had broken my heart to leave him and the feeling appeared to be mutual.

Flying gave me a lot of time to think. I did my best to put the dog behind me and focus on Ava. I came up with all sorts of hair-brained schemes to talk to her.

Maybe fly a banner in front of her window declaring my love. Or send a drone onto her balcony with a note to just please talk to me.

I was all for grand gestures, but none of them struck me right.

As my wheels touched down on the Houston runway, my phone chimed with text messages.

It was the training facility in Birmingham. Something had happened with Scottie.

Please call. We need to talk to you about Scottie.

How had the facility even gotten my phone number?

Baffled and worried that something had happened to the dog I had gotten quite attached to, I taxied over to the private terminal parking and went through the post flight checklist.

It was a hot day in Houston. Almost ninety degrees. According to most of the rest of the country and the calendar, it was autumn. But not here.

I'd moved on from thinking about Scottie and now they were reeling me back in. Probably wanted me to deliver him somewhere else.

Just what I needed. More time with a dog I was already attached to.

I was having enough trouble figuring out what to do about Ava.

With no excuses left, I dialed the number to talk to the facility about Scottie.

And just as I expected, I was on my way back to Birmingham to pick him up.

It just wasn't what I'd expected.

Chapter Thirty-Three

Ava

I'd just logged off of a Zoom call with a potential client, a very promising potential client, and walked to the kitchen for a drink of water. I felt good about this one. The client and I had seemed to just click. That happened now and then, even in business.

Sometime during the call, I'd slipped my feet out of my shoes so I was walking around my condo barefoot.

As I drank a glass of cold water, I thought about doing some Pilates. I had a new workout video that I wanted to try and I needed to do some stretches.

It was a hot October day and I was glad I didn't have to be out in it. I was especially glad I didn't have to be out in the traffic.

I loved working from home. If I had my way, I was never going back to an office job.

When my phone rang, I had to run back to my office to answer.

"Ms. Ava. You have a delivery."

A delivery. I was expecting a packet of paperwork to be sent by courier.

"Send it up please."

I dug my shoes out from under my desk and put them back on.

By then, the courier was at my door.

But the delivery was not the paperwork I had been expecting.

It was a delivery guy with a bouquet of red roses artfully arranged in a glass vase.

"What's this?" I asked the delivery guy.

"I just make the deliveries," he said. "Have a nice day."

"Have a nice day," I mumbled to myself as I closed the door.

Holding the flowers at arm's length, I set them on my breakfast table. Then stood back and looked at them. Twelve red dewy rose buds.

I couldn't quite wrap my head around why someone was sending me flowers.

I couldn't even remember the last time I had gotten flowers. To be honest, I wasn't even sure people still did that kind of thing.

It suddenly occurred to me that there was a card.

I yanked it off the little plastic stem and opened it up.

Meet me downstairs.

I recognized Austin's handwriting. Even after all these years, I recognized his handwriting. Meet me downstairs.

Like… now?

Of course he meant now.

I glanced down at what I was wearing. Jeans and a white button-down shirt. Perfect for a Zoom call. So at least I wasn't wearing my pajamas or my workout clothes. A few minutes later, I would have been dressed for Pilates.

It wouldn't hurt to meet him downstairs. He'd gone to all this much trouble to find me and to send me flowers.

I could meet him downstairs.

Two minutes later, I was on the elevator on my way down.

When I stepped off the elevator, a dog ran toward me. A dog I recognized immediately.

"Scottie? How are you here?"

Scottie barked once and started walking away from the elevator, then turned back and barked again.

"Okay, Scottie. I'll follow you."

I followed Scottie down the hallway to the lobby area.

Austin stood there watching me with amusement as he so often did.

Even though I'd known he would be here, it was still a shock to my system to see him.

"Hi," he said.

"Hi. How is Scottie here?"

"It's a long story," he said.

"I've got time."

We sat on the sofa, out of earshot of the concierge, and faced each other.

"I'm sorry Clara Miller showed up at your house," I said, getting that out in the open right away.

"It wasn't your fault. I saw her for what she was. We all know you weren't there to get my grandmother to sell her home."

"She did send me there for that. I told her I wasn't going to do it. I was just going to talk to Grandma. Then I was going to deal with the consequences."

"I know," he said. "I believe you."

"Your family?"

"My parents didn't know what to think, at first, but they know now."

"It was so wrong. What Ms. Miller wanted me to do."

"It's okay. I know."

I took a deep breath.

"So tell me why Scottie is here."

"That really is a long story."

I reached over and scratched Scottie's ears. He tried to lick my face, but being a cat person at heart, I pulled back. Then I found his collar.

"Wait," I said, leaning closer. "Why is your name on Scottie's collar?"

Austin grinned.

"He's my dog."

"But. Isn't Scottie a special guide dog?" Austin and I had already been through this, the first time I'd met Scottie.

"He is. But he has an eye issue that disqualifies him."

"A guide dog with an eye issue?"

"I know. The irony is crazy, isn't it?"

"It's serious?"

"Not really. But he can't be a working dog. So they retired him. To me."

Scottie barked twice.

"Why you? Does he need to go outside?"

"No. That's one bark. Scottie told them he wanted to be my dog."

"I won't even ask."

Scottie nuzzled Austin's hand until Austin petted him.

"We have a bond."

"I can see that."

"So," Austin said, turning his attention back to me. "Would you believe that I live ten minutes from here?"

"You do not."

"I do. Scout's honor."

"You were never in the Scouts."

"Driver's license?"

I held out my hand.

"Really?" But he pulled out his license and put it in my hand.

He really did live ten minutes from here and according to his license had for years.

"How is it we never saw each other?" I asked, handing it back to him.

"My guess would be because you never leave your condo."

"Good point."

"Feel like changing things up a bit? Having dinner with me tonight?"

"Okay."

"How about the next 36,500 nights?"

"I'm sorry, what?"

"I figure a standing date for the next hundred years will just about cover our time together, at least in this lifetime, what with modern medicine and all."

"Sometimes I wonder about you Austin Devereaux."

"Is that a yes?"

How could it not be?

"It's a maybe."

"Scottie and I are going to need more of a commitment than a maybe."

"Okay. Since Scottie is involved, it's a yes."

He really gave me no other choice.

I was, after all, already in love with him. Had been since seventh grade. Maybe longer.

It had been fate all along.

And if I had come to believe in anything, it was fate.

Epilogue

Ava
Two months later
The Sterling House

"CHAMPAGNE?" Austin asked, swiping two glasses from a passing formally—white tie formally—server.

"Thank you," I said. "That would be lovely."

Austin was wearing a solid black cashmere tuxedo. Long tails. White vest and white bow tie. By far the most handsome man in the room of handsome well-dressed men, I could barely take my eyes off of him.

"Have I told you how beautiful you look?" he asked as he handed me a glass of bubbly champagne.

"Hmm. About four times now."

"Let's make it five." His grin was intoxicating and the way he looked at me with those bright blue eyes...

I was wearing black, too. A long black cocktail dress with a sweetheart neckline and a white sash that tied in the back.

Smiling, I put a white gloved hand on his arm.

"The house is beautiful," I said. And it was. Marble floors. Chandeliers hanging from the tall ceilings.

The staircase itself was wide and curved. Just behind the stairs, tucked into the back corner out of the way was a five-piece orchestra. It was all very elegant.

And being December, it was decked out in elegant Christmas décor. A two-story tall Christmas tree adorned with simple clear lights and red ornaments. The shiny wooden rails of the stairway were wrapped with sparkly green and red garland. The orchestra played Christmas music.

Everyone who was anyone in Houston society was here beginning with the Worthingtons from Houston. And not just Houston either. The Ashtons from Pittsburgh were here. I'd even seen the mayor of Houston talking to someone across the room.

"Come," Austin said. "I want to introduce you to Noah and Savannah Worthington." Noah Worthington, the founder and owner of Skye Travels was here with his wife Savannah.

Austin led me through the crowded room to Noah Worthington, a tall distinguished man who lived up to his stellar reputation. He stood next to an equally sophisticated woman who didn't look a day over fifty.

My meeting with Austin's boss went much more smoothly than when he had met mine.

"It was such a wonderful gesture by your grandmother to

register The Sterling House with the National Association of Historic Places," Savannah Worthington said.

"She told me how much you helped with the whole process," Austin said. "That she couldn't have done it without you."

"It was my pleasure," Savannah said. "Your grandmother is a lovely lady. It was an honor to work with her."

"It's good to see Austin looking so happy," Noah said to me.

"They look good together, don't they?" Savannah said to her husband.

"Impressively so."

With one eyebrow raised, I looked up at Austin.

"Do you know something I don't?"

"I think we need to check on Grandma," Austin said.

"It was a pleasure to meet you both," I said as Austin tugged me away.

The music changed into something familiar.

"That song sounds familiar," I said to no one in particular.

"You might remember it from that day in seventh grade."

"What day?"

"Retro day."

"Oh. I remember retro day."

Austin put his arms around me and swept me into a little dance before I even realized what he was doing.

"You changed the trajectory of our lives that day."

"You mean when I kissed you?"

"Yes. One simple little kiss."

"Maybe," I said. "Or maybe it was all heading in this direction anyway."

"That's a rather deep thought," he said.

"I guess I'm a deep thinker once in a while."

He leaned me back in a dip.

"Just one of the many things I love about you," he whispered before he kissed me, then brought me back upright.

Still breathless from the dip and the kiss, I rather lost track of what was going on around us.

I glanced around, realizing that we were the only people dancing.

When my gaze swept back to Austin, I found him on one knee.

"Ava," he said. "Will you marry me?"

I stared blankly at him a moment. For some reason I was having trouble catching my breath.

Putting a hand over my mouth, I nodded.

He stood up and swept me around in a circle.

"Is that a yes?" he whispered in my ear.

"Yes," I said, feeling like my heart was going to burst.

"She said yes," he announced as he set me back on my feet.

Then everyone was clapping.

"We're getting married!" he said. "Right here." He turned to me. "Right here?"

I nodded again.

"Right here."

He swept me up off my feet again and carried me toward the back door.

"Where are we going?" I asked as he somehow opened the door and got me through while still carrying me.

"I'd like to kiss my fiancé in the moonlight," he said.

And he did.

He kissed me in the moonlight, sealing our fate forever.

Keep Reading for a Preview of
Stolen Dances and Big City Chances...

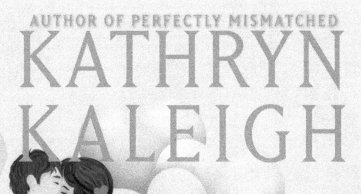

AUTHOR OF PERFECTLY MISMATCHED

KATHRYN KALEIGH

Stolen Dances and Big City Chances

THE DEVEREAUXS BELIEVE IN FATE SERIES

Preview

STOLEN DANCES AND BIG CITY
CHANCES

Chapter 1
Anastasia Devereaux

THE STERLING HOUSE was an iconic old-money Texas-style mansion nestled among flashy skyscrapers in downtown Houston. Texas-style in its 6000 square feet size.

It was decorated for fall which meant bushels of yellow and gold chrysanthemums in vases, tall and small, scattered all around the house.

Tall white pillar candles flickered on the fireplace mantle, the coffee table, and on wall sconces.

The music room was large enough for two elegant chandeliers, lights flickering, one on either side. Above the chandeliers, the ceiling was painted with golden etchings. Below the chandeliers, the polished marble floors reflected the flickering lights.

A lovely young lady in a formal maroon dress sat at the grand piano along with the rest of a four-piece orchestra. Their music echoed through the house.

Silvery sparkling maroon velvet curtains hung at the tall windows with darker burgundy toppers.

It was my brother Austin's wedding day. A beautiful day in the middle of October. A good time to get married in Texas—just after the weather stopped being miserably hot.

Not that he would notice the weather. He didn't see anything other than his bride. Everything was as it should be.

The morning ceremony was followed by a day of celebration before they left for the airport to board a plane for Paris.

I didn't envy him. He was only one year older than me, so we were almost like twins. I was happy for him and I liked his wife, Ava. Austin and Ava had dated in high school, then after going their separate ways for a few years, had taken no time picking up where they had left off. Engaged in December. Married in October.

The Sterling House was crowded with formally dressed men and women, boys and girls. They came for Austin's wedding, but I suspect many also came to see Sterling House.

Our grandparents had built it in another century and lived there until Grandpa had passed away. Grandma hung on, living here for another couple of years by herself, but she missed her family and had moved to Maple Creek to live with her son and daughter-in-law.

Investors had swarmed to buy the property for anything from a parking garage to a shopping mall. She, however, had gone a different direction. She had gotten the house registered with the National Association of Historic Places. Now Austin and Ava's wedding launched what would be a premium venue for weddings and other occasions.

As I walked passed an ornate gilded framed mirror, I almost didn't recognize myself. Recently graduated from college, I hadn't quite given up my wardrobe of jeans and t-shirts.

But today I wore a long chiffon maroon dress. And high heels.

Ava had picked me to be her maid-of-honor. Ava didn't have any family. Our family had been her family since she started dating my brother the first time. Back when they were in high school. I'd missed her during those years when they'd gone their separate ways.

Even now, the happy couple was doing something with cake.

I needed a break.

I stepped outside into the familiar backyard. We'd visited Grandma and Grandpa several times a year back when we were growing up.

It always seemed like the opposite of how most people lived. Most people went to the country to visit their grandparents and lived in the city. We lived in the country and visited our grandparents in the city.

We did all sorts of things in the city. We went to museums, plays, and baseball games. I had a particular fondness for downtown Houston, but I never pictured myself living here.

I preferred the quietness of the country. At least that was my excuse. The truth was, the thought of living alone made me sad.

I loved living with my family. Besides Austin, we had an older brother named Jonathan who was an overseas pilot. Jonathan was about seven years older than me and he only came home on occasions. Like today.

We all knew he was our parents' favorite child. It was okay. We all understood. I always saw Jonathan as being mysterious and interesting. Hard not to favor the mysterious and interesting one.

Then there were our two younger siblings. Theodore and Gwen. They were still in high school. A different generation. Our parents, it seemed, had their children in blocks of two, except for Jonathan. Maybe that was another thing that made him so different.

The maple trees had new green leaves. In fall, those leaves turned a beautiful red. Today in place of the bright red leaves, were tiny red twinkly lights. Someone must have come up with the idea of the red lights in place of the red leaves.

Out here the music sounded different. Faint. Like it was far away. And the conversations were barely audible at all.

If I closed my eyes, I could almost imagine myself back here as a child. When we weren't what Grandma called getting cultured, we played. Playing out here was different from playing at home because out here we were surrounded by skyscrapers.

At night, especially, the skyline around us was awesome. Every time the Astros had a home game, there were fireworks right there where we could watch them from our bedroom windows.

Even now I could hear the sounds of the traffic going up and down the streets. A police car, siren blaring, passed by, heading somewhere fast.

Without the sounds of the city, it would be easy to forget that Sterling House was in the middle of Houston.

It was for sure a different world from Maple Creek where we lived. In Maple Creek, the night sounds consisted of dogs and sometimes wolves howling in the distance. Crickets and owls. Not to mention the silent blinking of the lightning bugs.

There were no lightning bugs in downtown Houston. Not tonight anyway.

My grandmother stepped outside.

"There you are," she said. "I wondered where you got off to."

Grandma was an elegant woman in her sixties. Elegant, but easy to talk to. No one would ever suspect that she lived in a mansion in downtown Houston.

"I just needed to take a moment," I said. "To catch my breath."

"I understand," she said. "It's crowded in there, isn't it?"

"Very," I said.

"You know, Anastasia, weddings are supposed to be a good occasion for you to meet someone."

"Someone?" I asked with a little smile.

"Surely your brother has a nice friend you could spend some time with."

"I'm okay."

A red bird flew past and landed on the birdfeeder in the backyard.

"I thought you brought all the bird feeders when you moved in with us," I said.

"I must have missed one," Grandma said. "I worry about you."

I turned to face my grandmother.

"Why? Why are you worried about me?"

"You're what? Twenty-three?"

"Twenty-four."

"It seems like you should have started dating by now."

I laughed. "I've had dates Grandma."

"Yes. Yes. I know." She looked out across the twinkling lights of the maple trees. "But you should have a boyfriend by now. Someone to start sharing memories with."

Grandma sounded wistful. She and Grandpa had gotten

married when they were barely even legally old enough to marry at all. She had memories with him for probably fifty years.

I didn't want to hurt her feelings by telling her that people didn't do that anymore. That most young people waited until they were in their thirties to get married. By today's standards, I was still young.

Jonathan was thirty and he didn't even have a girlfriend, at least not that I knew of.

Austin was getting married, but he should have married Ava years ago. They had been fated together since they were in seventh grade. They were an anomaly.

The music changed and people were starting to dance.

"Do something for me?" Grandma asked.

"Sure, Grandma. I'll do anything for you."

She linked her arm with mine.

"Let's go back inside. And you." She patted my arm. "You find a nice young man to dance with."

"I don't want to dance, Grandma."

"Just one," she insisted. "Just dance with one young man. I want to see you having some fun."

"I am having fun."

She gave me a look.

"Okay," I said. "I'll see if there is anyone to dance with. But I can't make any promises that there will be anyone."

"Just look," Grandma said. "Looking is a good place to start."

"I'll look," I said, reluctantly.

"Good girl," she said. "Now let's go mingle."

I much preferred my own company, but I didn't want to disappoint my grandmother.

I would go and talk to my brother and his new wife. That was about as close to mingling as I wanted to get right now.

Hopefully, my grandmother would find something else to distract herself with and forget about me and my lack of social interaction.

I did not need a boyfriend right now. My career was just getting started. That was how it was done now. Grandma wouldn't understand.

Chapter 2
Christopher Taylor

I WASN'T SUPPOSED to be at what they were calling the wedding of the season.

One of the pilots who worked for Skye Travels, specifically for Noah Worthington's daughter, was getting married.

Noah Worthington was the founder and owner of Skye Travels, the private airline company he had started with just one little Cessna airplane.

It had grown quickly and was now a multi-billion dollar company. He hired his own family without shame. The only thing was they had to do in order to get hired was to be better than anyone else.

Since I was in no way, shape, or form related to the Worthington family, I considered myself fortunate to land a job flying for Skye Travels.

I was the only one in my graduating class fortunate to be hired by Noah Worthington. And I literally was hired by Noah himself. He might be getting up in age, but he still personally interviews every single pilot who goes to work for his company.

At any rate, I was the newest hire at Skye Travels and my mentor asked me to come along since his girlfriend was out of town.

I was hardly in a position to tell him I couldn't go. Not when I was just starting a brand new job.

So that's how I found myself at Sterling House, wearing a rented tuxedo, feeling exceptionally uncomfortable around hundreds of people I did not know, most of whom I would never see again.

I was just a regular guy—a pilot. I didn't attend fundraisers or other soirees unless I went as a client's guest. So I chalked today up to a work function.

The Sterling House was on the National Register of Historical places or some such. It belonged to Austin Devereaux's grandmother.

I'd lived in Houston my whole life, but I'd only been downtown a handful of times and I certainly didn't know that there was a mansion nestled right downtown among the high rises.

Like the other pilots, I drank a sparkling water in lieu of alcohol. I had a flight tomorrow and Noah Worthington had a very strict bottle to throttle policy.

One drink would get a pilot a warning. Two would get him suspended. And three would get him a trip to rehab. Or so I had been told.

I had a feeling getting fired was somewhere in there, especially for new guys.

So I stuck to sparkling water and no one thought a thing about it.

The little orchestra was set up in the music room, their music light and airy. It was happy music for a happy day.

"Come on," Frederick, my mentor said. "I'll introduce you to Austin."

Frederick had been a pilot for Skye Travels for right at eight years. He knew his way around the family and a fancy wedding at a fancy house didn't intimidate him one bit, even if he was more like me than he might want to admit.

Frederick was what I would call a flashy guy. He always wore a flirty smile, especially when he was around the ladies and he walked with what could only be called a swagger. A pilot's swagger.

Even now as we walked across the ballroom, he attracted attention. Every single female we passed checked him out. I kept track.

It wasn't that I cared. I was not a playboy. I'd had a couple of girlfriends, but I didn't date around. I didn't have a girl in every port or anything like I happened to know that Frederick did.

To each his own.

Although we were different in that way, we were alike in other ways. Like me, Frederick was an uptown boy. Uptown was by far a rougher area than downtown. The opposite was nothing more than a misperception.

"I think I met Austin once," I said, but I went along anyway.

"You can meet his new wife then," Frederick said, making his way through the crowd. We had to move carefully because people were dancing now. Waltzing to be exact.

Waltzing was most definitely outside of my purview.

Austin and his new wife were sitting together eating cake and laughing with each other. Now that was something I envied. My sister was married. They had one little girl—wrapped around my little finger—and another on the way.

That was the kind of lifestyle I wanted to lead.

As we neared the happy couple, a dark-haired goddess wearing a maroon dress came up and sat down right behind them. Her long flowing hair framed a heart-shaped face with red bow-shaped lips.

Frederick stopped in front of the couple and put a hand over his heart.

"Ava," he said. "You've gone and broken my heart."

Ava, apparently Austin's wife, just smiled.

"I have a feeling you'll bounce back just fine," Ava said.

"Go find your own girl, Frederick," Austin said with nothing but harmless amusement. "This one is mine."

"Fine. Fine. But first you need to meet Christopher Taylor. He's the newest Skye Travels pilot."

"Try not to pick up Frederick's bad habits," Ava said. "He will get you in trouble."

The dark haired goddess sitting behind them was watching Frederick in that way that women did. Like they couldn't take their eyes off of him.

Personally, if I was a girl, I would be turned off by his muscles. I was lean and in shape, but my muscles weren't cut. I didn't care to look sculpted. Flying was my gig.

"Nice to meet you both," I said. "And congratulations on your marriage."

"Are you from Houston?" Ava asked me.

The goddess sitting behind them leaned forward and whispered something to Austin.

"Yes," I said. "Uptown. Nothing like this."

Austin was shaking his head at the goddess.

"No," he said. "Not a good idea."

She whispered something else to him.

"Nothing wrong with Uptown," Ava said. "Have a sparkling water and enjoy yourself."

"I will. Thank you." I held up my glass of sparkling water and took note of the champagne glass in her hand. Austin was holding a glass of champagne, too. He wouldn't be doing any flying tomorrow, not as the pilot, at any rate.

"Don't say I didn't warn you," Austin told the girl sitting behind him, frowning.

"Frederick," he said. "This is my sister, Anastasia."

Frederick's face lit up like he'd just been given the keys to a brand new Phenom.

"Anastasia. What a beautiful name. For a beautiful lady. It's a pleasure to meet you." He held out a hand, but instead of shaking her hand, he brought it to his lips and kissed her palm.

I refrained from rolling my eyes, but barely.

Austin must have seen the struggle I was having. We exchanged a knowing look.

So the dark-haired beauty was Austin's sister. Anastasia.

And Anastasia had just been introduced to the biggest womanizer I had ever known.

Before I even caught onto what was going on, Frederick and Anastasia were headed out onto the dance floor where he pulled her into a waltz.

They looked good together. I had to give them that. But they were both pretty people in their own right. There was no way they couldn't look good together.

"What was that about?" Ava asked her husband.

"Something about Grandma," Austin said, keeping his gaze on his sister a moment longer.

"Well," Ava said. "I don't understand that."

"Unfortunately, I can't watch out for her," Austin said, cupping his wife's chin and placing a kiss on her lips. "It's my wedding day."

She smiled, then looked over at me.

"Good point. But maybe Christopher could look out for her."

"Whoa," I said, holding up a hand. "Frederick does what Frederick does. No offense to your sister."

"None taken," Austin said. "I'm far too familiar with Frederick."

"You have to do something," Ava said. "You can't just introduce them and not watch out for her."

"Anastasia is a grown woman," Austin said, then turned back to me. "Can you watch out for her? Just today. After that you're off the hook."

I hadn't known that going to a man's wedding meant I would have to watch out for his sister. That seemed like a task far beyond the call of duty.

"I'll do my best," I said.

What was a man supposed to do?

Offend a man at his wedding? Probably not a good idea.

Refuse to keep an eye on his beautiful goddess of a sister? Not a chance.

"Thank you," Austin said. "I owe you one."

"No problem."

"Nice to meet you," Ava said before Austin tipped her back in another kiss.

Looked to me like the two of them were far beyond ready to get started on the honeymoon.

Unsure what I was supposed to do now. What I was really supposed to do... I wandered over to the open bar and got myself a fresh glass of sparkling water.

Then I leaned back against the bar and watched the dancers until I caught sight of Frederick whirling Anastasia around the room. They weren't hard to locate. Not with her in her red dress.

"Excuse me," an older man, said as he came up to the bar. I stepped aside and looked around for another place to station myself with my unsolicited task.

I was beginning to see the value in learning to waltz. Maybe I'd check into lessons. Not that I would have all that many opportunities to waltz. Not in the ordinary world I lived in.

Still. It couldn't hurt. Working for the Worthington family, I never knew what I might be called up to do.

"Thank you Mr. Worthington," the bartender said. "Enjoy."

I hadn't recognized him at first, but that was THE Noah Worthington. Noah was a distinguished looking older man. He might have gray hair, but it only made him look all the more distinguished. A man could only aspire to be as successful as Noah Worthington and to remain as handsome with age.

Noah stood next to me. I couldn't tell if he was drinking champagne or sparkling water or maybe something else entirely.

"How are you Christopher?" he asked.

"Fine, Sir," I said. "A beautiful wedding."

"Those two should have been married years ago." He straightened. Gave a little shake of his head. "A familiar tale."

"How so?" I asked.

"I made the same mistake with Savannah. Got lucky when she took me back, though God only knows why she did."

"It was meant to be, Sir," I said.

He rocked back on his heels. "Can't argue with that."

"Is Ms. Worthington here?" I asked.

"Yes," he said. "Excuse my bad manners. Come on. I'll introduce you."

"You don't have to—"

But Noah was already walking away, obviously assuming I would follow.

He was a man who expected men to follow him and they did. I'd yet to meet anyone who didn't admire Noah Worthington or an employee who wasn't loyal to him.

I had met a few people who were envious of him, but none who wished him ill. I'm sure they were out there—there was always someone—but I never let a conversation go down that direction. I hadn't worked for him long, but I had, it seemed, already fallen into that loyalist camp.

He was charmed as far as I could figure.

Any man who could take one little Cessna airplane and turn it into a billion dollar company was the epitome of success, definitely admired by pilots all across the country.

I followed Noah through the crowded ballroom, past half a dozen men who greeted him. Past dancers on the ballroom floor.

As instructed, I kept one eye on Anastasia as Frederick swept her around the dance floor.

Noah stopped in front of two beautiful women, one clearly older than the other. They stood, their heads bent together, deep in conversation, but as we approached, the older woman looked up and smiled at Noah.

He kissed her on the cheek in a show of affection, most men of his station wouldn't dare in this type of formal setting.

"Savannah," he said. "This is Christopher Taylor. He's one of our newest pilots."

"It's a pleasure to meet you, Christopher," she said. "Welcome to the team."

"It's an honor, ma'am."

Savannah turned to the woman standing next to her.

"This is our daughter Ainsley. She runs our animal transport department."

"Hello Christopher," Ainsley said. Ainsley was tall like her father and had her mother's features. She looked as good as expected, coming from two good-looking successful parents.

"Be careful," Savannah said. "She'll try to recruit you."

"As long as it involves flying," I said.

Noah clapped me on the back.

"Spoken like a true pilot," he said.

"You have to love animals," she said. "It's a lot different from flying human passengers."

"I can only imagine."

I caught a glimpse of red as Anastasia swept past in Frederick's arms.

I couldn't help but watch them as they passed. It was my job, after all.

"We've got to do something about that," Ainsley said.

"Ainsley," Savannah said. "It's not our business."

I couldn't pretend to know what they were talking about. It sounded like they were talking about Anastasia, but I had no way of knowing if that was a correct assumption.

"Are you two still talking about Anastasia?" Noah asked, verifying my suspicions.

"It's our duty," Ainsley said.

"It's not our business," Savannah insisted.

"Anastasia Devereaux is the granddaughter of the owner of this building—The Sterling House," Noah told me.

"Austin's brother."

"Yes," Noah said. "You know her?"

"I can't say that I do, but..." How much did I want to disclose? This was my boss. I had no reason to hide anything from him. "But Austin asked me to look after her tonight."

"See," Ainsley said. "Even Austin is worried about her."

"He did seem worried about her," I said. "But it's his wedding day..."

"It's Frederick," Ainsley said. "Everyone knows he can't be trusted around women."

They were all three looking at me now. Noah, Savannah, and their daughter Ainsley.

"You've got to break in there," Ainsley said.

"Break in there? What does that mean?" A sense of panic was settling into my stomach and I was beginning to regret coming here tonight.

"She means cut in," Noah said, then added at my blank expression. "Cut in and dance with her."

Now I really was going to be sick.

"Sorry, Sir. I don't dance."

"Everyone dances," Ainsley said, dismissively.

"Ainsley," Savannah said with the tone only a mother could use.

"Just walk up there, tap Frederick on the shoulder, and take his place. He has to give her up."

"Do people still do that?" Savannah wondered, looking over at her husband.

Noah glanced around the room at the dancers.

"It might be a little old-fashioned."

"It might be very old-fashioned."

"Who cares?" Ainsley said. "We can't stand by and let Rebecca Devereaux's granddaughter's reputation be destroyed."

She had a good point, but I didn't see how sending me in was going to change that. Anastasia might not even want to dance with me. As far as I could tell, she appeared to be having a good time with Frederick.

Not surprising. Frederick had a way with women that I would never understand.

"Daddy if he won't do it," Ainsley said. "You will."

Noah looked at his daughter. Shook his head.

"And that would look how?" he asked.

"I told you it's not our business," Savannah said. "Anastasia is a grown woman."

Ainsley put her hands on her hips and glared at no one in particular.

Then she turned her gaze back to me.

"You have to do it," she said. "It's Austin's sister."

I was shaking my head.

No matter how much regret I was having right now, it was too late to take dance lessons now.

I'd been tossed into the deep end by the Worthington family.

I had more than a feeling that no one told them no.

I could be the first.

Preview

STOLEN DANCES AND BIG CITY
CHANCES

Chapter 3
Anastasia

I WAS ONLY DANCING with Frederick to make my grandmother happy.

It was just a side benefit that all the other women at my brother's wedding gave me envious glances as he swept me around the ballroom.

Just a side benefit.

And Frederick had smooth moves. The way he looked at me like I was the only woman here tonight was a heady feeling.

But it was only to make my grandmother happy.

I caught a glimpse of her as we swirled past. She should have been smiling. I was, after all, only doing what she'd asked me to do.

She'd asked me to find someone and dance with them. Just one dance, she'd said.

I was already into my third dance with Frederick and right about now, to be quite honest, I could use a glass of cold water.

But Grandma wasn't smiling. She was talking quite seriously with a woman I recognized as Savannah Worthington. Savannah Worthington was Noah's wife. Noah Worthington. The owner and founder of Skye Travels. My brother's boss.

Why would they be talking? And why did they keep glancing in my direction?

I realized, a bit belatedly, that Frederick had asked me something.

He'd already asked me three "Would you rather" questions. None of them had answers that made any sense and I was quite honestly getting weary of them.

"I'm sorry," I said. "I didn't quite catch that." It was easy to blame the music and conversations swirling around us for my lack of attention.

"Would you rather be able to shrink down to the size of an ant or to grow to the size of a skyscraper?"

"Excuse me?"

Frederick laughed and repeated his question.

"I don't know," I said. "A skyscraper, I guess."

"Why?" He deftly swept me past a pair of dancers, people I didn't recognize.

"So I could see a long way off I guess."

"I'd rather be able to shrink down like an ant," Frederick said.

"Why?" I asked, but the whole question made no sense to me.

"So I could slide into someone's pocket and listen in on their conversations."

"That sounds rather underhanded."

He looked a little offended. How could he be offended by that? He'd started the whole ridiculous conversation.

"I'd like to stop," I said. "For a glass of water."

"Sure. We should finish out this dance though."

"I really don't—"

We turned and someone tapped Frederick on the shoulder.

Thank God. Someone was cutting in.

"What?" Frederick asked.

"I'm cutting in," the man said.

I recognized the man as the one who had been introduced by Frederick as Christopher.

"You can't just—"

"Actually," I said. "He can."

I somehow removed my hand from Frederick's arm and put it on Christopher's. Not an easy move while we were dancing.

"Whatever," Frederick said, with obvious annoyance, letting me go.

As he walked away, Christopher and I stood still, my heart racing from all the dancing.

"Thank you," I told Christopher. "Can we just get something to drink? A glass of water?"

"A glass of water?" Christopher asked. We were standing in the middle of the dance floor now, neither one of us moving. "We can most definitely get a glass of water."

I was so thirsty, I thought I imagined the look of relief on his face.

He tucked my hand in the crook of his arm and led me off the dance floor toward the bar.

As we passed my grandmother and Mrs. Worthington, they both smiled at us.

"I'm Christopher," he as we took our place in line at the open bar.

"I know. I'm Anastasia."

"I know," he said. "You're Austin's sister."

I nodded. Considered.

"What made you come to my rescue?" I asked.

"Did I? Come to your rescue?" he asked. "You seemed to be having a good time with Frederick."

"Thirsty," I said to myself. "I needed a break."

"I see."

We reached the bar.

"Two glasses of ice water," he said.

The bartender slid over one glass, then another.

I took mine. Drained it.

"Can we get a refill?" Christopher asked.

"Sure thing." The bartender refilled my glass and handed me a cold bottle of water to go with my glass of water.

"Thank you," I said.

"Let's find a place to sit down."

"Yes. Let's." Sweeping my hair back off my neck, I followed Christopher to a sofa in the study next to the ballroom. I felt like I had just finished a cardio workout.

After we settled onto the sofa, I opened my bottle of water and filled my glass again.

"I think I made Frederick mad," I said.

"I wouldn't worry about him if I were you," he said.

"Why not?"

He nodded toward the door. Frederick was walking outside with a woman I didn't recognize.

"Well," I said, looking away.

"Do you mind?"

I shrugged. "I just met him. Doesn't do much for my ego though."

"Your ego doesn't need him."

I looked over at him sideways. "You're friends with him, right?"

"Frederick is my work mentor. So friends? Not so much."

"Good." I poured the rest of my water into my glass, the cool water sparkling over the ice cubes.

"Can I get you some more water?" he asked.

"Maybe in a few minutes. I'm okay for now."

"Just let me know."

"How do you know Austin?"

"I just met him."

"Ava?" Ava didn't have any family, but she did have friends, mostly work friends.

"Just me her, too."

"You just came with Frederick."

"That's right," he said.

"What made you cut in?"

"It's a long story," he said. "I'll tell you after we get to know each other better."

I smiled and although it was a simple statement that probably meant nothing at all, it was simple statement that gave me butterflies.

It was a simple declaration that he wanted to get to know me better. Somehow that pleased me.

My grandmother had insisted that I dance with someone. I'd almost ignored it, but I really would do anything for my grandmother.

When Frederick showed up, seeming to know both my brother and his wife, I'd called in a favor. One of many favors my brother owed me.

I should have heeded his warning about Frederick, but the way Frederick kept glancing at me told me that he would be willing to dance with me. It would make my grandmother happy.

How was I supposed to know that once we started dancing he wasn't going to let me go? I wasn't sure which was worse. That he wouldn't let me go or that he kept asking me stupid "what if" questions.

"Can I ask you something?" Christopher asked.

"Please don't ask me a what if question."

"Okay. I won't." He took a sip of water and frowned at me. "I don't really know what that is."

"Then yes." I smiled over at him. "In that case, you can ask me a question."

"How is it you're the most beautiful girl here tonight?"

"You can't ask me that," I said, leaning toward him, keeping my voice low.

"Why not? Is it a what if question?"

"No." I laughed. "You can't because it's Ava's wedding."

"Oh. Well. I wasn't counting her. That's a given."

I smiled. My grandmother just might have been right after all.

Maybe it didn't hurt to meet someone to spend a little with after all.

Preview
STOLEN DANCES AND BIG CITY CHANCES

Chapter 4
Christopher

IT WAS A WELL-ACCEPTED fact in some circles that when a man met the woman he wanted to spend his life with he knew it immediately.

Although I had no reason to either believe it or not believe it up until now, I was quickly becoming a believer.

Anastasia was absolutely enchanting.

I'd known it the moment I first saw her. When she sat near her brother and his wife and got her brother to introduce her to Frederick.

Music befitting a wedding, sometimes happy and sometimes

heartbreakingly romantic, swirled through the air. It blended with laughter and conversations.

Three photographers roamed the house, someone always staying focused on the newlyweds. They were going to have thousands of pictures to choose from. I did not envy them that.

"Why Frederick?" I asked.

Anastasia took a deep breath. Shook her head a little.

"It's a long story," she said repeating my words back to me. "I'll tell you after we get to know each other better."

I laughed. "Deal. You know. I don't think I've ever been to a morning wedding before."

"My brother had to be different. Actually they're flying to Paris tonight. I think. Their flight got rescheduled and they already had the wedding planned."

"That explains it," I said. "One of my friends in college had a wedding party that lasted two days."

"That seems a little extravagant to me," she said. "Seems like a wedding is something to do and get on with it. Small and quick."

She really was a woman after my heart.

"I couldn't agree more."

"You're not into big weddings?" she asked.

"I don't think I'm suited to big weddings."

"Why not?" She set her glass down on the end table and pulled her hair loose around over one shoulder.

"It's not something I should tell you," I said.

"Well. Now you have to tell me."

"That's how it works, isn't it?"

She gave me a little smile. "Of course it is."

"It's not a secret, so I guess I might as well tell you."

She leaned forward, one eyebrow raised.

"You've got me imagining all sorts of things," she said.

"I don't know how to waltz." There. I'd told her. It had to be told even if it meant she never spoke to me again.

She looked blankly at me as though trying to comprehend.

"Is that it?" she asked.

"That's it."

"That's not a good reason, you know."

I waved a hand in the direction of the ballroom. "Seems like a pretty good reason to me."

"It's fixable," she said. "People take lessons all the time."

"I'm going to have to look into that."

We sat in silence a few minutes while the music changed again. This time it was back to a romantic tune, but with a happy beat to it.

"But you cut in. You were going to dance with me."

"That's part of that long story I'll be telling you in a few years."

"A few years," she said on a little laugh.

"Yeah... Maybe. If then."

"Well. I won't let you forget," she said with a little smile that lit up her enchanting big green eyes. The way she was smiling at me made her eyes look like a green forest after a rain.

"No," I said, unable to look away from her. "I wouldn't think you would."

I figured I had a definite advantage as far as her memory went. I would always be the guy she met at her brother's wedding.

And as for me... She would always be the girl I fell in love with at first sight.

. . .

Keep Reading *Stolen Dances and Big City Chances...*

Kathryn Kaleigh writes sweet contemporary romance, time travel romance, and historical romance.

kathrynkaleigh.com